I0691734

Short and Sassy

BY

ERICA THOMAS

ISBN: 978-0-692-14770-2

Dedication

TO LOVERBOY, THANK YOU FOR BECOMING A PART OF MY LIFE. IN THE TIME I NEEDED YOU, THE JOURNEY WITH YOU BROUGHT THE BEST OUT OF ME, EMOTIONALLY AND SPIRITUALLY. THANK YOU FOR CALLING ME BABY'S MAMA. THOSE TWO SIMPLE WORDS IGNITED THE STORY, BIRTHING OUR BLESSINGS, WHICH HELP ME TO CREATE THIS BOOK OF SHORT STORIES. FROM AN IMAGINATION BURIED DEEP YOU UNLOCKED THE CREATIVITY IN ME BY SPOKEN WORDS. THANK YOU AGAIN, KDM

CONTENTS

ACKNOWLEDGEMENTS

Special thanks to Margaret Diehl who did the editing, excellent job. You added so much to the stories. To George Leslie, thank you for your contributions; to Explosive News Print Shop who did my book covers, video, bio, and synopsis for my book, you made it easier for me, although you did all the hard work. I am so thankful for you guys. To Mac Williams, thank you for taking the time to read every story before print. Your honest feedback encouraged me to keep writing, and the second book is in the making.

This has been one interesting journey. Some stories are emotional, and I found myself being the character as if I were there. You can really get lost in writing, that's what makes it surreal. Keep me writing. Feedback is good; you be blessed.

Reach out to me at mystiquedvision@gmail.com

Again, I say thank you…

FOREWARD

According to Wikipedia, muses are defined as, "inspirational goddesses of literature, science, and the arts in Greek mythology. They were considered the source of the knowledge embodied in the poetry, lyric songs, and myths that were related orally for centuries in these ancient cultures."

As I read through Ms. Thomas's draft copies of her first book, the muses of centuries past came to the fore. With each story, I found myself wanting more. Her musings made me smile; they made me contemplate; they made me introspectively think of my own life, relationships, decisions that I have made. Lastly her stories caused me to reflect back on the days of my youth and ask myself the question: if I only knew then what I know now....

I think that you will have similar reactions; enjoy the read and just wait on her next book.

Mac J Williams

BIRTHING OUR BLESSINGS

Traffic was always hectic at 5:00pm. When you work those types of hours, that's to be expected. Instead of driving into that chaos, Camille decided to wait it out, grab a bite to eat at the diner on the corner. She strolled in, grabbed a booth, looked at the menu. She glanced up to see a young man checking her out.

He was cute, nicely dressed, smooth black skin, hair looking like manicured grass—oh, maybe she did more than just glance at him. Her eyes went back to the menu. She looked up again. He was standing in front of her. He introduced himself.

He said, "Hello, my name is Dale."

Camille replied, "Hello. How are you?"

"I'm fine. I'd be even better if you told me your name."

Camille said, "How important is to you?"

"How important?" Dale replied. "If we are going to be dating, I need to know what to call you when we're out."

Camille replied, "You sound confident!"

"I am."

"I'm impressed."

1

Dale asked, "Do you mind if I sit down with you?"

Camille replied, "No, I don't mind."

Dale said, "What brings you into the diner; you're usually on your way home around this time." She looked at him like *what the hell?*

Camille asked, "How do you know that?"

Dale replied, "You'd be surprised what I know about you."

Now she was really curious. Camille asked, "Since you know so much, what's my name?"

Dale said, "Your name is Camille."

She almost spit her water out. "If you knew my name, why did you ask me for it?"

Dale said, "I wanted to see if you would give me the right one."

Camille replied, "But I never gave you my name."

Dale said, "No, but your reaction says I am right."

"You've been doing some research on me!"

Dale replied, "Just enough!"

Camille said, "Just enough for what?"

Dale replied, "Just enough to know I'd like to know more about you."

Dale had Camille's complete attention now. The waitress came to take their order; they chatted a little bit more, exchanged numbers, and Dale paid for her dinner. He said, "Are you in a hurry to go home?"

Camille replied, "No, not really."

2

"Would you take a stroll in the park with me? It's a beautiful night for one."

Camille replied, "Sure, I'll take you up on that offer."

They walked over to the park. Sat on the bench by the water. They talked about their careers, goals, likes and dislikes. The conversation turned into hours of enjoyment. It was getting late, and Camille had to get home; she had to be to work early in the morning. Dale walked her to her car. He told Camille to text him when she got home, so he knew she made it home safely. As soon as she got home, she texted him. He texted back, "Thank you for coming to the diner; you made my night." They talked, video chatted, emailed, texted— you name it, they did it.

It was soon getting serious. He'd stay at her place. She was staying at his. They bonded quickly. They didn't rush into anything. They weren't intimate until six months later. One night over dinner, Dale said to Camille, "I think I'm in love with you!"

Camille replied, "You are, Dale."

Dale smiled. "How do you know that?"

"For one, I'm in love with you, and two, you said it in your sleep."

Dale said, "I tend to talk in my sleep."

Camille laughed and said, "Yes, and I tend to watch you in your sleep."

They both laughed, and he kissed her on her forehead. "I do love you, Beautiful."

Camille replied, "I love you too, Handsome!"

They made love in front of the fireplace that night; it was emotional. A month went by. Camille missed her cycle. Dale and Camille had never talked about having children. Well they had; it just wasn't on their to do list for now. She made an appointment at the doctor's office. The test came back positive; she was pregnant. Camille didn't know how Dale was going to take the news. She didn't tell him right away. She wanted to wait until he got home. She started dinner. Dale came in from work. He kissed Camille on the cheek.

Camille asked, "How was work today?"

Dale replied, "It was good. And how was yours?"

Camille replied, "It was good, washed the car, gassed it up, got my nails done, found out I'm pregnant, and we are having spaghetti for dinner!"

Dale said, "Hold up, back up, you found out what?"

Camille said, "I'm pregnant!"

Dale said, "For real you are?"

Camille said, "Yes, I am!"

Dale said, "Okay. We are having a baby!"

Dale had this big grin on his face. Camille was happy; he was happy.

In the third month, Camille started cramping. She used the bathroom and saw spotting. She woke Dale up to tell him what

4

had happened. They rushed to the hospital. By the time they put Camille in the room, she felt a plug of water gushing out of her. She had had a miscarriage. She was devastated. So was Dale. He comforted her.

Dale said, "This happened for a reason." She said that she knew that, but she wanted to have his baby. She loved Dale very much. She wanted a part of him. The hospital kept Camille overnight for observation. Dale stayed with her. In the morning they went home. Dale told Camille to rest, not to go to work, he would wait on her if she needed anything, and she agreed. She went to bed, lying there thinking about what just happened. Dale came in the room, knelt by the bed, and asked Camille was she okay.

"Not really. I really wanted to give you a baby."

Dale replied, "I know, baby, I wanted it too." He wiped her tears. "Baby, it's going to be okay. I promise you it will be."

She sat up and hugged him. "You 're such a good supporter. I thank you for your strength."

Dale said, "I love you, Camille. I will always love you. I will always be your strength, your supporter, your provider, and your husband."

Camille said, "Husband?"

Dale said, "Yes, baby, husband." He slid the diamond ring on her finger.

"Before you say anything, I want you to hear my heart," Dale said. "When you told me you were pregnant, I wanted to do things the right way. I wanted to marry you right away. I wanted our child to come in this world and have my name, but we didn't. I don't know why our baby was taken away from us so soon, but before we have another one, I want you and my baby to have my last name. Camille, marry me, baby, I love you. I want to marry you."

Camille felt a burst of emotion. "Yes, baby, I will marry you."

Dale stroked her cheek and kissed her softly. Camille took his hand and put it on her stomach. She said, "One day I will give you a part of me."

"You promise?"

"Yes, baby, I promise."

Five months later Dale and Camille got married. They did it small. They married at the courthouse. They were in the process of buying a home and they didn't need extra expenses. They invited a few friends as witnesses and after the ceremony, they went out to dinner—simple and elegant. They were both happy. Dale booked a little getaway to Jamaica. Camille needed to get away; she was under enough stress. She needed to relax.

Their room was absolutely beautiful. It had silk window drapes on the door. Camille opened the doors to the balcony. The wind had the drapes flowing like they were waving. They had a room by the beach; the smell of the water and the breeze was heavenly. There were rose petals on the floor around the bed. The sunset from their view looked like a blazing orange. It made the night complete.

Dale carried Camille over to the bed and lay her down; he reached into his bag to get a bottle of oil.

Camille asked, "What is that?"

Dale replied, "It is blessed oil. I had my pastor bless this oil. I told him that we lost our baby, and I asked him to bless this oil so that I can rub your stomach. I don't want to lose another baby, Camille."

He took the oil and rubbed Camille's stomach. He prayed and rubbed the oil at the same time. Dale said, "I'm going to passionately make love to you tonight; I'm praying that you carry our baby full term because I love you." Camille saw the desire in his eyes. She fell in love with Dale all over again. He did just what he said he would do; passionately and seductively, he made love to Camille. They hadn't made love since the miscarriage; he wanted her to heal from that, physically and emotionally. Through the night making love was the only thing on their agenda.

Jamaica was breathtaking, and the weather was steamy. The water and sand felt good on Camille's body. She lay in the water taking in the waves and the scenery. It was just what they needed. Dale took good care of Camille, as always. He was a good husband, and she knew one day he'd be a good father.

As quickly as it started, the honeymoon was over. They returned home.

A month in, after moving into their new home, Camille missed her cycle. She didn't want to panic. She made an appointment. She was pregnant again, and she was excited. She couldn't wait to tell Dale, but there was so much going on. He had just gotten a new promotion at his job and was working long hours. When she got home, he was asleep. She didn't bother him. He looked so handsome. She was hoping their baby looked like him.

In the morning, she cooked Dale breakfast. She called him down, so he could eat. He sat at the table. There was a folded note by his plate. He opened it up, it said, "Good morning, Daddy; I will see you in eight months." Dale looked around for Camille. She was standing in the hallway looking at him reading the note. He went over to her.

Dale said, "My baby is having my baby!"

"Yes, I am!"

He knelt down and kissed her stomach. He said, "You're taking a leave of absence from work. I make enough money for the both of us; you are going to be on bed rest for the remainder of this pregnancy."

Camille said, "Are you sure?"

Dale said, "Yes, we are not losing our baby!"

Dale hired a maid. He made sure Camille didn't lift a finger, except to answer the phone when he called to make sure she was resting.

Camille was on bed rest; she didn't have to cook, clean, or anything, Dale made sure of that. He called her every chance he got, to see how she was doing. Her meals were bought to her. The only time she left the house was to go to doctors' visits; other than that, she was at home. Every night when Dale came home from work, he would kiss Camille's stomach, sing a Jamaican song to the baby, and then rub oil on her stomach and pray. He did that every night, up until her due date.

Dale catered to Camille; she deserved it. Dale knew her body had been through something from the miscarriage. He massaged her swollen feet, propped her pillows and rubbed her back. From ice cream and pickles, to tomatoes and mayonnaise, he was there for her. She was thankful for him. It was getting close to the due date. Dale was working on the nursery. The ultrasound confirmed they were having a boy. Dale wanted a boy. She wanted to give him one too.

Two weeks before the due date, Dale was home with Camille. He had taken off from work, so he'd be home with her when she went into labor. She was having unusual pain. It wasn't contractions. She didn't want to alarm Dale. She turned over and over to get comfortable. She felt that pain again. She sat up. Her water broke, and she woke Dale up. "Baby, it's time!"

"Time for what?"

Camille yelled, "Baby, my water broke!"

9

Dale jumped up. Grabbed the packed bag, helped her get dressed, and then ran downstairs. He returned five minutes later.

Camille said, "Where did you go?"

"I took two shots of Patron. I want to be in the zone!"

Camille laughed. "It's time to go, baby. This pain is excruciating!"

"How far apart are the contractions?"

Camille said, "They're more than contractions!"

Dale said, "What do you mean?"

Camille couldn't explain it. "Let's get to the hospital, hurry!"

They called their next-door neighbor to drive them. Dale got in the back seat with Camille. She didn't want Dale to drive anyway; he'd just had two shots of Patron.

They arrived at the hospital. Camille was rolled into the Labor and Delivery. Nurses prepped her for delivery, and Doctor Johnson asked Camille how she was feeling.

Camille said, "I'm in a lot of pain!"

Doctor Johnson said, "Let me see how far you've dilated." He opened her legs. The head had already crowned.

Doctor Johnson said, "Camille, I need you to push. Your baby's head has crowned. When I say push, you push. Are you ready?"

Camille said, "Yes, I am!"

The doctor said, "Push." Camille pushed. Dale was holding her hand and looking at the same time to see the birth of their son.

Camille pushed, but she was having that unusual pain again. The doctor said, "We are almost there, push!"

"I can't. It hurts to push." She was panting and sweating.

Dale looked at Camille. "What's wrong, baby?"

Camille replied, "I'm having this pain in my rib area. Every time I push, I feel this pain!"

The doctor came over to feel the area. He said, "There's something wrong—you have a lump under your rib cage."

"What kind of lump?" Camille and Dale asked.

The doctor replied, "I can't say. It could be a tumor. Camille, you are going to have to push—this baby has to come out!"

Camille said, "No, I can't. It hurts!" Camille's blood pressure started to rise.

Dale looked at Camille and said, "Baby, push!" Camille started to cry.

The doctor said, "You have to!"

Camille said, "No!"

Dale said, "Baby"!

Doctor said, "Camille, push!"

Camille replied, crying. "No, it hurts."

Dale and the doctor said, "PUSH!"

Camille screamed, "NO, WAIT!" The room became silent.

Camille took Dale's hand and placed it on her stomach. She placed her hand on the lump area under her rib, and she began to pray, "Lord, this pain hurts so bad, I don't know what it is. I don't know what this lump is, but you do. I believe you will move everything that is hindering me from birthing our baby. You have the power to remove all sickness and disease. I believe your word and what you say is true. Move this; my baby needs to be born and this pain is keeping me from pushing. MOVE IT NOW. In your name I pray, Amen." Camille felt a peace in her spirit. She felt the lump move, slowly. Dale could see the flesh of her belly ripple. Whatever it was that was going on, it was happening slowly.

The doctor said to Camille, "How do you feel?"

Camille replied, "Doc, I feel like pushing."

Doctor Johnson said, "I'm ready when you are. Push, Camille." She started pushing. "Almost there—one more good push. Push, Camille, push." She pushed, and her baby boy was born. The doctor called, "Nurse, hurry, come quick come get the baby." The nurse hurried and grabbed the baby!

Camille said, "What's wrong? Is my baby okay! Please tell me that my baby is okay. Dale, please go and see that our baby is okay."

Dale ran over to check on the baby. The nurse showed him the child and said, "He's fine. You have a healthy baby boy."

Dale said to the doctor, "If my baby is healthy, why the sudden rush for the nurse to take him?"

Camille said, "What's wrong, tell us!"

The doctor looked at them both and said to Camille, "You're going to have to start pushing again." Dale and Camille looked at each other. The doctor said, "When I say push, give me two good pushes. Are you ready?"

Camille replied, "Yes."

The doctor said, "Take a deep breath, Camille, and push." Camille pushed. "One more time—you're almost there, Camille. Push!" She gave it one good push and another baby boy was born. The doctor said, "Congratulations, you birthed two healthy baby boys. The other baby was up under your rib, that's where that pain was coming from. I had to turn the baby around; he was in a breech position." Camille looked at Dale. He was so happy he was crying.

Dale said, "I wanted a boy and now I have two!"

Camille looked at Dale and said, "Because you anointed my belly through my pregnancy, we now have twin boys."

Dale said, "I had a dream that our first child was a boy. I believe God gave us twins because we lost the first one."

Dale looked at Camille and said, "You are so beautiful."

"I wanted to give you a boy, and now we have two. Those are your boys, Dale, you are going to be such a good father to them. They are blessed to have a father like you. I'm so glad I was able to give you what you desired."

"I thank God for giving you to me, Camille, and birthing our blessings."

13

TEARS ON MY WINDOWPANE

The rain was comforting. Angie glanced over at the window. Tree branches brushing against the window; that's what woke her up, that and the thunder. It had rained all weekend. Angie was on vacation. She had just come home from a cruise. She was supposed to go on it with Robert; it just happened to not work out that way.

Lonely days and nights. It had been two months since their breakup. Robert was one of those guys you'd always want to be around. He'd make you laugh. He'd catch Angie off guard—she had more food come out of her mouth than stay in it. He should have been a standup comedian. Robert was naturally funny.

Angie could see a future with Robert. They were completing each other's sentences. She pretty much knew how his day was going to be before he'd start it. They were compatible in every way; they complemented each other. They looked so good together. So, what happened? If everything was good, what went wrong? Love! That's what went wrong. She fell in love with Robert, and he didn't fall the same way she did. They had been together for a year. She thought that was enough time to grow on each other and express feelings. Instead, they would get into arguments. They could never decide on anything, except what they were having for dinner. Angie was catching feelings. He knew it; he was catching something but wasn't professing it to Angie.

Angie loved everything about Robert. She liked his suave style; she loved the way he dressed. He had a neat way about him. She liked him in gray sweatpants; they were made for his body. They fit him just right. All his clothes looked like they were made just for him; he knew what to buy, and they had to fit a certain way, nothing loose. He was just fine; she'd sit on the bed and watch him put on every piece of clothing. She noticed everything about Robert—his walk, the way he ate, the way he held his pen when he wrote, the way he talked and responded; she was all in. His skin was chocolate. His cologne would saturate it; the chemistry in his skin made his scent smell like aromatherapy; she'd lie on his chest and stroke it and inhale the aroma. She did that on nights they would talk; she felt so happy and relaxed.

Conversations would be very detailed. Most of their talks took place in bed. Robert had a seductive way of getting Angie's attention. In the middle of the night if he wanted to talk, he'd slide his finger down the crease of her back. She'd arch it every time he did that. She knew when he did that, he wanted to talk, and it was important. They used to have some good conversations.

But when she expressed her feelings towards Robert, he would turn it into an argument. She couldn't understand why he would flip the script on her, but he did. Angie knew if it would always be that way, there was no point in continuing the relationship. If the feelings were going to be one-sided, with her loving him, and him not giving it back to her, she'd rather be by herself. She talked to Robert about it, and they agreed. The decision was made; they went their separate ways. Angie hadn't heard from Robert since. No calls, no text messages. Angie thought, *he doesn't miss me.*

When the phone rang, she checked it: a missed call from Jamie. Jamie was Angie's best friend and Robert's sister. She had introduced Angie to Robert; she thought they'd make a cute couple. She thought she was Cupid's sister. Jamie sent a text saying she was coming over in the morning. Angie was a hairstylist; she owned her salon. On Mondays, she was closed. Jamie was the only one who could come to her house and get her hair done.

Angie had a three-car garage with one of areas set up as her salon. In the morning, it was still storming. Angie wondered why Jamie would come on a rainy day to get her hair done. The doorbell rang. Angie answered the door, and said, "Girl, of all days, why come on a rainy day to get your hair done?"

Jamie said, "I didn't come for that."

"What did you come over for then?"

Jamie walked up to Angie and gave her the warmest hug. Jamie said, "I think you needed that. I know you miss Robert. I can't give you the hugs he gave you, but I know you needed one."

Angie responded, "Thank you, Jamie, I really did need that. I miss Robert—I miss him badly. Does he talk about me, mention my name, pull out a picture or anything?"

Jamie responded, "Girl, you know he's so reserved, he doesn't express his feelings. I think my daddy is a mule because Robert is as stubborn as one."

They both laughed. "I bought you some homemade chicken noodle soup."

Angie responded, "I'm not sick!"

"I know. But it's a rainy day, and that's the best time to make a pot of soup, so I bought you some over."

Angie said, "That's so thoughtful of you. Next time you get your hair done, it's on me. Jamie smiled. Angie said, "You want to stay for a while?"

Jamie said. "No, I have errands to run, but we'll be in touch." She hurried to her car. It was pouring rain. Angie waited until Jamie got in her car and pulled out before she closed the door. Angie went in the kitchen and ate the soup, which was so good; it was hearty. Angie needed that too. A hug from Jamie and soup, the best combination ever. Angie finished her soup and went back upstairs. She walked over to the window sitting area, plopped down on the pillows, propped her feet up, grabbed a blanket, pulled back the curtains and looked at the rain fall.

She remembered when Robert's car would pull up. She'd be so happy; she felt like a schoolgirl with her first crush. The rain on her window reminded her of the tears running down her face when Robert left. It was painful; the rain were her tears, and the windowpane was her face. Angie watched the rain until she fell asleep. The thunder woke her up; she had slept about an hour. It began to rain harder. She had trash to put out.

She went downstairs, gathered up all the trash, hit the button for the garage door to open and saw car lights. At first, she thought it was Jamie. The lights went off, and he stepped out of the car. It was Robert. Angie's heart started pounding, thinking, *how did I miss him coming up the driveway? He must've driven up as I was coming down the stairs.* He slowly walked to her, grabbed the trash, and put it in the dumpster. He came back and said, "I came to pick up the rest of my things."

"That's fine." Her heart was saying, *please stay.* They hadn't talked or seen each other in two months; it was best to let him come get what he still had there, so they could have closure. Whatever she felt in her heart wouldn't be said. Robert went upstairs to the bedroom. Angie followed him. He had those gray sweatpants on; she could've fainted. Why would he come over to get his things and wear those sweats? He could've worn jeans. He was such a teaser.

18

He began to pack his things. She turned on the TV to watch something, anything, to hold back the tears. Robert saw her attention wasn't focused on him. He packed everything and said he was getting ready to go. Angie wanted him to stay. Even if he said no, at least she'd asked. With all the strength she had in her, she took a deep breath and said, "The weather is really bad out. At least stay until it lets up."

Robert replied, "Yeah, okay."

He said he would stay a while since it was a long drive and he was tired anyway; he had just gotten off work. Angie smiled; she was happy but nervous. What would she feel tomorrow, having gotten another taste of him?

They watched TV until they fell asleep. Hours later, she was awakened by his finger going down the crease of her back. When she woke, she knew he wanted to talk. She heard the shower in the bathroom running, she so slowly turned around to look at Robert. The light from the TV hit his eyes—they looked like lit candles dancing in the moonlight. She had never seen anything like that before.

Angie said, "What's the matter, Robert?" Tears began to flow down his face.

Robert replied, "Come with me."

Robert took Angie's hand and ushered her into the bathroom. Robert stepped into the shower, and then said, "Please join me in the shower." Angie couldn't say no. She stepped in with him, and he caressed her body sensually. Robert washed every inch of Angie's body seductively. Every area he touched, she gave him a response. He liked how she responded to his hands and fingers. After the fifteen-minute hot shower, he towel-dried Angie, and escorted her back into the bedroom.

He said, "I've always loved you, baby."

Angie had to adjust her ears to hear him clearly. She wanted to make sure she was hearing him right.

"You changed everything about me. I was losing myself. I was so scared; this had never happened to me before. I had to snap back to me. I stayed away but the more I stayed away, the more I was missing you. Forgive me, Angie, I didn't mean to hurt you. I know I did; I came over because I saw your tears on my windowpane. I saw your face on my window, crying in pain. I felt your pain. I couldn't grasp what you felt for me, but now I know I need you in my life. I'd be foolish to let you go.

"I'm in love with you. I've been in love with you. I always knew it. I carried you in my spirit, so you were always on my mind. I missed you so much. I missed your beautiful smile, your touch, the scent of your perfume on your body, your lips. Can I kiss them, baby, please, baby, can I kiss them? He slowly grabbed Angie's face, kissed her mouth passionately.

When the kiss was over, Angie said, "Did you really come over to get the rest of your things?"

"Truthfully, I asked Jamie to come over to see if you were home. She knew I missed you; I told her I was in love with you.

20

Jamie was happy to hear that. After she left you, she texted me to let me know you were home.

"I knew we hadn't talked or seen each other in a while. I knew you weren't seeing anyone; I felt that in my heart, and it was confirmed in my dreams. I knew your heart was only beating for me. You love me deeply beyond my soul, Angie, and I know the way you love. You love forever. Tonight, I don't want to make love to you... I want to intimately hold you in my arms. This is our beginning. Until the very end, you are my always and forever Angie...Good night, baby..."

HIS LAST WISH

Driving into the airport terminal, Tonya was thinking, *Wow, it's been forever since I've seen Larry.* He had been her best friend since they were kids; they had gone everywhere together—movies, skating, amusement park; they even went to each other's prom. They were inseparable; he was her hanging partner, her protector, like the brother she never had. He ran all the guys away. She thought that was cute. He moved away when he went to college, but they always kept in touch. They both got married and divorced around the same time. How ironic.

She knew they would have a lot to talk about. Tonya pulled up and parked to wait for him. She must be nervous; her hands were shaking. She said to herself, "Girl, get it together. He's your best friend, not your ex-boyfriend." She took a deep breath. She composed herself. There was a knock on the window. It was Larry. She got out of the car. He looked like he had lost a few pounds, but it looked good on him. She gave him a hug. He kissed her on the cheek.

Larry said, "Baby girl, you look good." He gave her that name. She was younger than he was; she was always his go-to girl.

Tonya said, "You lost a few pounds."

"Yes, it's this new diet I'm on."

"Well, you look good."

"Thanks."

He put his luggage in the trunk. They got in the car, and he smiled at her. He turned on some smooth jazz. They both had the same taste in music. He reclined his seat back, closed his eyes and vibed off the melody. Tonya found it quite odd that they didn't talk; what was on his mind? He'd tell her in his own time. They pulled up to her house. She showed him the guest room. He said, "You did something different to the room."

Tonya said, "I remodeled and painted it your favorite color. This is your room every time you visit." She thought he'd smile, thank her, but he had a distant look on his face.

Larry said, "I want to lie down for a few. I'm a little tired from the trip."

Tonya said, "Okay. Is there anything you need?"

"I have everything I need. I have you, my best friend." The way he said it—Tonya got a chill. *Don't imagine things,* she thought.

Tonya said, "If you need anything, I'll be down the hall." She closed the door. She went into her room to catch up on some reading. A few hours later, she heard the shower running. She knocked on the door to make sure he had found the towels and everything he needed. Her eyes widened. She gasped, speechless. Larry said, "Baby girl, let me explain. I don't know what you're thinking and how you're feeling but let me explain." Tears began to well up in her eyes.

Tonya said, "Please tell me." He took her hand and put it on his chest.

Larry said, "What you're touching is a port. It's a tube attached to my chest for chemotherapy. Baby girl, I have stage 4 colon cancer. I left the clinic right after my treatment and caught the next flight out to come see you, my body was rejecting the chemo. They wanted to try a different treatment, but I didn't want it. What I did want was to come home. You were always home to me. I knew I was home when I got in the car; your presence was better than the chemo. I felt at peace, I knew where I needed to be for the remainder."

Tonya said, "Wait! What? What do you mean remainder?"

Larry said, "They gave me three months to live."

Tonya dropped to the floor. She said, "I can't believe what you're telling me." She thought, *this tall, handsome, talented, vibrant man is dying; my best friend is dying.* She played it over and over in her head in disbelief. She was shaking and crying.

Larry said, "We are going to make the best out of these three months if you allow me to stay. I need to be with my best friend."

Tonya replied, "You never have to ask me that question. This will always be home to you." He kissed her on the cheek. She left the bathroom. Went to her room, fell on her knees and began to cry out to God. She was devastated. She cried so hard that night, she fell asleep on her knees.

The next morning, they went to church. Larry had a good time. He hadn't been to service in a while, but the spirit was high, and he felt it. After church, they went out to eat. He didn't have much of an appetite, but he was good company. They took a ride through the park. Sat by the water, reminiscing about good times. They talked about their failed marriages and their career success. Tonya loved the sound of his voice. He would be a good narrator for stories and movies. She could listen to him all day. Occasionally, his conversation was interrupted by coughing. He sounded frustrated when he'd try to talk and cough at the same time. The cancer was spreading, but Tonya wanted to make his remaining days the best of times.

On certain nights, they'd go to the movies, other nights out for ice cream. One evening they went to the beach to look at the sunset; it was beautiful, and he enjoyed it. Two months passed, and he was starting to become frail. Nights going out stopped. They stayed home and watched movies. He would fall asleep on the couch. Tonya would grab his favorite blanket and cover him up; she'd sit across from him and watch him drift in and out of sleep.

Tonya had to be strong for him. She wouldn't cry in front of him; she'd go in her room. Larry started to sleep downstairs because he was too weak to climb the stairs. Tonya would check on him through the night. At times she would be awakened by his moaning. He'd be in pain, but he wouldn't let her comfort him. He was always strong. Anything he went through, he'd do on his own. She respected him for that. One night, Tonya heard this light knock on her bedroom door. She opened the door. Larry said, "I'm in so much pain I can't do this any longer." He fell into her arms, and they fell on the floor. He was moaning and crying, he was in so much pain.

Tonya said, "Can you get up on the bed?" He couldn't. She said, "Lay your head in my lap if you can." He did. She called the paramedics. Her prayer shawl and oil were close by; she grabbed them, anointed his head with oil and covered his body with the prayer shawl. She began to pray for Larry. Tonya was crying and praying. Larry's body was shaking. He was in so much pain. She was holding him and praying. *God, please take this pain from him. Please, Father, take this pain away from him.* She had never seen Larry cry before. Tonya couldn't imagine what he was going through. His tears were unstoppable, and his moaning sounded excruciating.

Tonya said, "Larry, don't you leave me. Please don't leave me!" His body wouldn't stop shaking. Tonya screamed. "God, please!" Suddenly, peace descended. His moaning began to quiet; she started to feel his body relax. Tonya heard the doorbell. It was the paramedics. She said to Larry, "You're going to be fine. The paramedics are here." She heard no response from him. She shook him; he didn't respond. The doorbell rang again. He had a tranquil look on his face. She tried to wake him again. "Larry, wake up! Wake up, please!" Nothing.

He was gone. Her best friend had died. She sat there looking at this handsome man. He was gone. She carefully laid his head on the floor and ran downstairs to let the paramedics in. She told them where he was; she stayed downstairs. They were up there for about fifteen minutes. Two men came down to get the stretcher. Minutes later, they brought him downstairs. A sheet was covering his face. Tonya screamed! She knew he was gone. She had to see him again. She removed the sheet from his face. Kissed him on his cheek. She watched them as they carried him away and put him in the ambulance.

Tonya sat on the step and cried like a baby. Her best friend was gone. She couldn't believe it. She grabbed her phone, began to call family and friends. She made arrangements with the funeral home. His funeral was a week later. It was beautiful; everyone that knew him had so many nice things to say about him. She knew all that was said about him was true. After the funeral, they took his body to be cremated; that's what he wanted. He also wanted Tonya to keep his ashes. Larry said he'd always wanted to be near her. She sat in the car to wait for them to bring the urn of his remains. She didn't want to go inside.

Tonya looked over his obituary. She shed tears. She was glad he wasn't in pain any more. But sad he was gone. They bought the urn to her in a box. She went home, took the urn and put it on her dresser where she could see it every day. She went into his room and sat there. She grabbed one of his shirts and lay in his bed. She slept there all night. In the morning, she left his room. She didn't touch anything; that was his room, and she left it just the way he did. She missed him, missed him so much. A week later, Tonya

27

went to the mailbox. She saw a letter from a lawyer's office. It requested her to come into the office for the reading of Larry's will.

A couple of days went by. She went into the law office; they took her into a room and said, "Let's begin."

Tonya said, "Wait a minute; are there any other people coming? Shouldn't we wait for them?"

The attorney said, "No, you're the only beneficiary."

"Okay."

"He left you a substantial amount of money. He wants you to start a foundation in his memory. He would also like you to donate money to certain charities; all the amounts are in the envelope." The lawyer handed Tonya the sealed envelope.

She opened it. There was a check in her name for twenty-five million dollars, checks for the charities and one to start the foundation in his memory. He also left her property and assets. She'd had no idea he was so wealthy. She remembered Larry would always say, "Baby girl I will always take care of you." He stayed true to that promise. Tonya did just what Larry wanted her to do for the charities and other organizations. She started the cancer foundation and named it His Last Wish Foundation, In Memory of Larry Dubois.

FOUR MINUTE DRIVE

Finished up with the architect, Janet went to look at the one-acre lot she'd bought a month ago. She wanted to look at it again before construction started tomorrow. She was finally building her dream home. She had always wanted to build one, and she had saved up for years. Janet had been looking at this property for some time. When the time was right, she bought it.

One thing she didn't want to do was build the house alone. She wanted to be married, build it together with her husband. Unfortunately, that didn't happen for her. The man she loved had her in standby mode. The relationship wasn't moving into something serious; that wasn't on his agenda. Janet and Derrick had been dating two years. Everything was going smooth, and then they hit a rough spot—she wanted more of him, and he was giving less of himself. They were spending less time together, having fewer phone calls, less conversation, and she started to feel just like that, LESS.

Janet had poured all she had into him, heart, mind, body, soul, and spirit. She liked the vision she saw with him, but he didn't see the same thing. After a while, she felt like she was pursuing him, instead of him pursuing her. She'd reach out to Derrick; he'd respond, tell her everything was good between them, and then the next day, nothing; she wouldn't hear from him. Days and weeks

29

went by, not one phone call from him. She made up her mind she wasn't chasing after him.

Time was of the essence. Janet was on her way out of town. Her friend and mentor, Melanie, was having a conference in Maryland, and she needed her to assist. Janet needed to be on the road by 12:00 pm to get a good start. Since Derrick wasn't calling, there was no need to let him know she was going out of town. Janet's girlfriend Wendy lived in the area, and she would be overlooking the construction while Janet was away.

Janet had made preparations for the time she'd be away—for six months, until the house was ready. She would be visiting Philadelphia to see her family while she was in Maryland. She gassed up her car and was on the road at exactly 12:00 pm. She'd have plenty of time to think about what she wanted to do when she returned to Florida, whether she wanted to continue the relationship with Derrick or just stay single for a while. Melanie called Janet during the drive.

"Are you on the road yet?"

Janet replied, "Yes I am."

"I sense something is wrong with you; do you care to talk about it?"

Janet said, "I'm feeling a little down. It's Derrick."

"Yes, I know, but we talked about that. He will come around. You just have to focus on you right now; you have to work on yourself. You are a broken woman, and you need to heal so you can love him, whole and totally, not in broken pieces. Neither of

30

you are ready for each other. He needs to heal as well, but he has to know that for himself. He's hurting from past relationships; two broken people can't love each other the right way. Give yourself time, give him time, and everything will work out for the best."

Janet felt so much better after that. Melanie encouraged her; she knew her situation. Janet was glad God had given her someone who knew exactly what to say when she needed it. Janet stopped a couple of times to get gas and something to eat, trying her best not to think about him. She got into Maryland about 1:30 am. She checked into the hotel and slept like she was in a coma. Driving by herself tired her out.

Morning came. Ring, ring; it was Melanie. She asked how she slept.

Janet responded, "I slept like I could sleep some more."

Melanie laughed and then said, "Get another hour of sleep, then join me for breakfast around ten. We can go over details of the conference. I'll give you the address where we will meet."

"Sounds good."

Janet went back to sleep. An hour later, she woke, dressed and headed out to breakfast. On her way out, she got a call from her daughter, Jasmine. Jasmine said, "Mommy, how was the drive, did you make it safely?"

Janet said, "The drive was fine. Sorry I didn't call to let you know."

"It's fine. I'm glad you made it safely. Guess who came by the house?"

"Who?"

"Derrick!"

Janet asked, "What did he want?"

"He wanted to know where you were. I said you went out of town for business. He asked when you were coming back. I told him I didn't know."

Janet was shocked that he'd come by. She hadn't spoken to Derrick in two months. Jasmine said, "He looked like he wanted to say more, but I wouldn't be much help to him, because I'm not you. I wouldn't give him any information about you. He looked sad, Mommy, like he lost his best friend."

Janet thought, *now he knows how I feel. He's at a standstill; he doesn't know what's going on. He can't get in touch with me.* Janet had left her main phone at home and took another one. Only certain people had that number; Derrick was not one of them. If he was calling, the only voice he was hearing was the voicemail. Janet had his number, but she wasn't calling him. Janet had another call coming in. She said to Jasmine, "I have to go. I'll talk with you later."

She clicked over. It was Melanie wanting to know if she was coming to breakfast.

Janet said, "Yes, I'm on my way."

Janet arrived at the restaurant. She saw Melanie and greeted her. "I apologize. My daughter called, and I got caught up in the conversation."

Melanie responded, "It's fine, I just wanted to make sure you were okay. You're in a new state; I didn't want anything to happen to you."

"Thank you for your concern."

"I would like for you do praise and worship; I know you can sing."

Janet replied, "I am honored, and I will do as I am led to."

"That's why I asked you to come, because you are obedient."

"That's the only way to be. What time does service begin?"

"The service is tomorrow. It starts at 7:30 pm."

"Perfect. I will be heading out to Philadelphia later today and will return tomorrow for service."

Melanie replied, "Look forward to it. God speed to you on your travels."

"Thank you."

They ordered breakfast, and Janet paid the tab. She went back to the hotel to pick up her overnight bag and then headed out to Philadelphia. She called her mom to let her know she was on her way. During her drive, she thought about Derrick, then she thought about what Melanie said, that she needed to heal. Hearing his voice was not going to make it better; she needed time away from him. He didn't need to see Janet; he needed to see what he was missing in himself.

Janet arrived at her mom's house. Her mom was just preparing lunch. "Hello, Mother," Janet said.

Her mom replied, "Hello, dear." They embraced. Her mom said, "Janet, you look like something is on your mind."

"You know your daughter well."

"What's on your mind, love?"

"I'm in a where-do-I-go-from here mindset."

"Where do you want to go?"

"Wherever my heart takes me."

"You answered your own question. Follow it like a map, don't U-turn or detour. That's your GPS. Follow it until you get to your destination."

Janet replied, "Thank you, Mommy, I know I can always count on you."

"You already had the answer; you just needed confirmation."

Janet smiled. She ate lunch with her mom, then headed up to her room and took a nap. Hours later, Janet woke up, checked her phone. Wendy had called. She returned the call. "Hey, Wendy, what's going on?"

"Everything is good here. Construction started; I'll send you pictures as it goes along."

Janet replied. "I appreciate that."

"Talk with you later."

Janet hung up the phone with Wendy. She thought about Derrick. Her heart wasn't detouring; it was heading straight for him. Janet shut it down quick. She didn't feel his love. Her heart didn't lie; she wanted it too, but it wasn't going to happen. Janet rested. She was tired from all the driving, so she didn't get up until the next day. She went downstairs to have breakfast. She needed to be back on the road to Maryland, so she ate, kissed her mom goodbye and was back on the road.

She returned to Maryland just in time to get a nap and change for service. As she was led, Janet sung from her spirit. Praise and worship was intimate; it flowed the way it was supposed to. After she sung, she prayed. It wasn't on the program, but that's the way Janet flowed, and it set the atmosphere. Janet was called to be a minister. She ran from that calling, but it was catching up to her quick. The service went just the way it was supposed to go, unrehearsed.

After service, Melanie wanted to talk to Janet.

"I saw you in a vision with your husband."

"I'm not married."

Melanie replied, "No, not yet. Your husband is Derrick."

"Really!"

"Yes, while you're away, he is being worked on. In his dreams, he is being told not to touch you unless he marries you. Janet, you are a pure vessel that is not to be tampered with. Only certain hands can touch you, and they can't be dirty. Dirty hands belong to men who want to make you a girlfriend or side chick; clean hands belong to the ones that want to make you a wife.

"Only clean hands can touch you, Janet. Those hands belong to the one that is ordained to take care of you. You were created to be a wife. So, while he's being prepared to be your husband, you

35

prepare yourself to be his wife. In due time, your hearts will be mended as one, but for now, you both must heal to become one. For the remainder of your stay here, let me prepare you, minister, and equip you, so that you will be ready for him."

As the months went by, Janet was back and forth between Philadelphia and Baltimore. Melanie prayed and mentored her. Janet felt stronger and more confident; she felt she could face Derrick, for whatever he had to say. The day before she left, she called Jasmine to say she will be back tomorrow, to help Wendy with the housewarming party; she gave her a list of people to invite and the time of the event. By the time Janet would get home she wouldn't have to rush and do anything.

Janet packed up her things. She stopped by to see Melanie before she left. Melanie prayed for Janet for safe traveling and gave her blessings for her new life. The ride back to Deland, Florida, was quicker than the trip going. Her mind was more peaceful.

Janet returned home on Thursday, she loved her new home; Wendy had done an excellent job with the furnishings. Jasmine welcomed her mother with a hug and kiss and handed her the other cell phone.

Janet turned the phone on. She saw twenty-five missed calls from Derrick. She didn't call him right away; she will wait until Saturday. She rested Friday and thought about calling Derrick. That thought came and went fast, but it was lingering. Saturday evening came, and the place was beautiful. The event was starting at 7:30. Janet called Derrick at 7:00 pm.

Janet said, "Hello, Derrick."

Derrick responded, "Hello, Janet, how are you?"

"I'm doing well. Listen I'll be in your town for a few hours. My friend is having a housewarming party. It would be nice to see you; I'll be heading back out tomorrow. The party begins at 7:30pm. I'll text you the address."

Derrick replied, "You're going out of town again?"

Janet said, "Yes, I've been busy. Hopefully I'll get to see you before I head out." She hung up the phone.

Derrick saw it was 7:18pm. He hurried up and got dressed and put the address in the system. He didn't want to miss seeing her. He started up his car, backed out of the driveway, and when he saw how long it was going to take him to get there, he laughed so hard he almost cried. A FOUR-MINUTE DRIVE; he couldn't believe it. He drove down the street and around the corner. He saw all the cars parked outside. He found a parking spot and headed in.

There was so much food, drinks, music; it was a warm and cozy atmosphere. Janet was sitting on the sofa talking with company. She saw Derrick, acted like she didn't see him, turned her head and started laughing. He walked over to her and kissed her on the cheek. She said, "Hello, I see you made it. Make yourself comfortable, there's plenty of food to eat." Everyone was mingling, lots of laughter.

The party ended around 9:30pm. Janet walked everyone to the door. Derrick stayed behind. He wanted to talk. Janet said goodnight to the guests, closed the door, walked back to the living room where he was sitting. Derrick was beginning to realize he didn't even know who his hostess was. He looked around but didn't see anyone. Maybe the woman had gone to bed already. Maybe she trusted Janet to lock up. He said, "What time you heading back home?"

Janet took off her shoes, let her hair down and replied, "I am home!"

Derrick said, "What do you mean? This is your home?"

"I mean this is my house."

"Are you serious?"

Janet replied. "Very!"

"You live right around the corner from me."

"I know. When you first invited me to your place months ago, I fell in love with this area, so I started looking for houses. I saw this lot for sale, so I bought it.

"Why didn't you tell me?"

Janet said, "Let me ask you a question before I answer yours. How did you feel when you went to my apartment and couldn't find me, couldn't get in touch with me? How did it feel, Derrick?"

"I felt lonely, lost and confused."

"That's the same way I felt when we were together."

"Why didn't you say something to me?"

"If you were into me, you would have picked up what I was feeling."

Derrick said, "At one time I could do that with you. I almost knew what you were thinking. I felt so connected to you, Janet, when we started talking, and then somehow, I felt separated from you."

Janet said, "What happened?"

"I happened. It was me; I pulled away. You were going at a speed I wasn't ready for. I pumped the brakes, so you could slow down."

Janet said, "I'm sorry. You should have said something."

"I tried to, but you weren't listening. The way you love, Janet, you shut down everything but your heart, so even if I whispered it in your ear, you still wouldn't have heard me. You can't help how you feel."

"I loved what we had. I knew where we were going. Once you stopped calling me, I felt like you weren't interested in me any longer."

"I will always be interested in you. I just didn't want to move too fast and make the same mistakes as I did before; I didn't want us to make mistakes together. I cherish you, that's why I wanted you to slow down. So, tell me, Janet. How did you come about this location—why this area?"

"I wanted to be close to you. I was looking at this location for a while, and it was a good price. I bought it nine months ago. My girlfriend supervised the construction while I was out of town."

Derrick replied, "I saw the construction going on, but I had no idea it was yours."

"Yes, it's mine. Would you like a tour?"

"I sure would."

Janet showed him around, and he loved the house.

Derrick said, "You have good taste. I like your walk-in closets, and you have two of them."

Janet replied, "Yes, one for me and one for my husband if I ever get married." Derrick smiled.

"I'll have to buy you a housewarming gift. Well, let me go, I have church in the morning. It was good seeing you, Janet."

Janet responded, "And you as well."

Janet walked Derrick to the door; he honked as he pulled out. She cleaned up the kitchen, blew out all the candles, and went to bed. An hour or so later, she heard the doorbell ring. She opened it. It was Derrick. He said, "I had to come back."

"Why?"

Derrick replied, "A husband and wife should never live in different houses."

Janet said, "What do you mean?"

"Janet, you know you're my wife."

"What makes you think I know that?"

Derrick took out his phone, and said, "Call my wife." Janet's phone rang. Janet had this surprised look on her face. She grabbed her phone and answered it, Derrick said, "Hello, Janet," smiling at her. She hung up the phone quickly.

Then she walked up to Derrick and did something that confirmed everything; she whispered, "Call my husband," and Derrick's phone rang.

Derrick said, "So does this mean we are setting a date?"

Janet said, "It looks like it."

"After our first date, instead of your name I put my wife."

Janet said, "I knew you were my husband when I was out of town. Melanie said I would get confirmation when I got home; she didn't say what it was." Janet's phone rang; it was Melanie.

Melanie said, "Can I tell you what will confirm he's your husband?"

Janet said, "Yes."

"When he gives you the ring."

As soon as Melanie said that, Derrick took it out his pocket. Janet said, "OMG."

Melanie said, "He showed you the ring?"

"Yes, he did."

Melanie said, "Blessings to you, daughter."

Derrick said, "You are my wife, Janet. He put the ring on her finger."

She said, "Yes, I am."

Derrick said, "I'm going home now. I wanted the night to end with you knowing that you are going to marry me. I tossed and turned so many nights with you on my mind, not knowing where

41

you were, no way of contacting you. I was missing you deeply. Now that I know where you are—besides in my heart—I can peacefully sleep now. Can I call you in the morning? Maybe we can go to breakfast and start setting a date."

"Yes, Derrick, I would like that."

He kissed her on the forehead and said, "Goodnight, my love."

LOVE COLLISION

Being stuck in traffic on Sunday morning was not what Denise had had in mind. She had left early enough not to run into five o'clock work-week chaotic traffic. She had spent the weekend hanging out with friends, celebrating their wedding anniversary. She was anxious to get home; the traffic crept like a tiger after its prey. Time didn't stand still; she did. She'd been in it for an hour until it stopped, nothing moving. Denise saw people getting out of their car, walking down to see what the holdup was. She locked up her car and started down the side road.

"BANG"! Denise didn't see the car coming. It hit her so hard, it threw her fifty feet from the scene. Everyone ran to help. The man that hit her jumped out of his car to assist. He said, "No one touch her; I'm a doctor," and he called for the paramedics, not knowing that ahead there was a multiple accident, and the road was blocked. The ambulance arrived, and the doctor assisted them. Denise was put on a stretcher. The doctor asked the paramedic what hospital they were taking her to, and he wrote down the information.

The traffic began to move. He noticed one car had no driver in it, and he knew it must belong to the young lady who was in the accident. When the police came, he explained what had happened. They looked for witnesses to the accident, but traffic had started

43

moving and nobody had stuck around. They told him they'd have to talk to the victim. He made sure he knew where her car was being towed. Then he drove to the hospital to check on the young lady. He didn't know her name. Since he knew the hospital personnel, he didn't have any trouble getting her name. The nurse at the front desk said, "She's in surgery. She has a broken arm and leg, fractured ribs, and a concussion."

The doctor was in a daze. He couldn't get past the name—he knew that name. Back in college, he knew that name. Could it be the same lady? He had met her freshman year; they struck up a conversation waiting in line to register. She was studying law, and he was studying medicine. His parents were both doctors, so he kept that career in the family. Denise came from a single-parent home. Her mother depended on the government, but she always had potential to be someone greater than the environment she grew up in.

It had been about fifteen years since they'd seen each other. He knew what floor she'd be on if she was being operated on now, and he took the elevator to the fourth floor, then peeked into the operating room. The surgeon said, "David, you're back so soon"! David was a surgeon at the hospital. He had been on his way to visit his mother when the accident occurred. David had called his mom to say he wouldn't be able to make it; something urgent had come up, and he would visit her next weekend.

"Is she going to be okay?"

The surgeon said, "She will be fine. Is she a patient of yours?"

44

"I hit her with my car."

"Man, I'm sorry. For both of you. Yeah, she'll be okay."

David was relieved. He looked at her with sorrowful eyes. She lay there with tubes in her mouth, all because of him not paying attention. *How could I be so careless,* he thought. David stayed at the hospital while she was in surgery. He went to get a bite to eat, made a few phone calls. When he returned, he was told they had moved her down to the third floor. She was in room 304. How ironic; that was her dorm room in college.

They would cram for tests together. David would go to Denise's room. It was quiet. He had a bunch of loud roommates, who didn't respect the fact that he had goals and had to study to achieve them. David would call Denise up, explain the situation, and if she said it'd be okay to come over, David would study until he fell asleep. Denise was that chill girl. David liked her style; she was a tomboy. She had a different walk in certain shoes; she'd wear low and high-top sneakers, with sweat suits.

She had swag about her. Unique. The way she'd walk in stiletto heels would make a man howl like a wolf on a full moon. Yeah, she was bad; she had this gangster walk about her. Her walk said a lot about who she was. She always had a way of breaking things down. David liked to hear Denise break down a conversation like a math problem. She'd make trigonometry look like arithmetic. Nothing complicated, always easy to understand. She had David's attention; he just never told her.

David glanced in the room to see how she was. She was peacefully lying there. Although she looked bruised, she was beautiful as ever. There was nothing more David could do. He asked the ward nurse, whom he knew well, to call if anything changed.

Days went by, and there were no changes. She had swelling on the brain, so it was going to take a little time for her to come through. David had so many questions to ask her. Would he be facing criminal charges? Would she forgive him? Did she even remember him? All kinds of thoughts went through his head. David tossed and turned that night. There were no changes. What he did, did it make matters worse?

Midnight hour. David finally got the call he'd been waiting on, three days later. She had finally woken up. David got out of his bed so quick, you'd think he'd overslept and was late for work. He hurried to the hospital. He walked into the room and quickly walked out. There were two police officers in there asking questions. His heart was beating like it was running a marathon. He went into a panic mode. He stood in the hallway, listening to them asking questions.

David's hands were starting to sweat; he had to maintain his composure. The questioning was over, and the officers left the room. He saw them walk down the hall. David didn't want to go in just yet. He took a deep breath. Suddenly, he heard, "You can come in now, David." David's heart jumped. He thought, *how did she know it was me?* He slowly walked in the room with a startled look on his face.

"How are you doing, David?"

"I'm doing just fine. I need to ask how you're doing."

"I'm am well, and I forgive you."

David said, "For hitting you?"

Denise replied, "Sit down let me talk to you."

David took a seat right next to her bed. Denise said, "When your car hit me, our eyes met. I saw the horror in your eyes. It all happened in slow motion. I knew those eyes; I had seen them before. I knew it was you." David's heart was pounding so hard, he thought it was going to jump out of his chest. Denise said, "Calm down!" *Did she see my pulse racing?* David thought. Denise said she told the police it wasn't his fault. She shouldn't have been out of her car. It wasn't a hit and run; she knew David was there. She doesn't know how she knew, but she knew.

Denise said, "Once I saw your eyes, David, after you hit me, I knew you wouldn't leave me there alone. Parts of me are broken, but I will heal." Denise made this visit so much easier. David had all kinds of thoughts in his head. She made it all go away, as she used to make a trigonometry problem look like arithmetic; she really made it easier for David.

Denise asked, "How's your mom and dad doing?"

David replied, "My dad passed away some years ago. He had retired from the practice. He had a heart attack about three years

47

ago, passed away in his sleep. Mom is doing well. I visit her as often as I can, I call her every day."

"Sorry to hear about your father. What about you, David?"

"What about me?"

"Did you get married? You have any children?"

"No wife, no kids. I do have a dog. What about you, Denise? What's going on in your life?"

Denise stared off for a minute, then she replied, "I'm in an abusive relationship, been trying to get out of it, but he seems to find me everywhere I go. I have a restraining order against him where I live; anywhere else I go, he seems to find me. But I'm glad all is well with you, David." She tried to prop herself up. David gladly helped her. Since she had a broken arm, she couldn't really move around.

Denise said, "You still wear that cologne." She smiled. In college, Denise always knew when David was around; his cologne would be lurking in the air. Denise would look around for him, but he'd be gone. That scent would linger, like it stayed there just for her. David looked at her with amazement. He couldn't believe she remembered. It was soothing to his soul. They talked many hours about their college years and their lifestyles now.

Denise had her own law firm. David could tell by the Bentley she was driving, she was doing just fine.

David said, "It's late, you need your rest, I'll come see you later this morning."

Denise asked, "Do you have to go? I'm enjoying your company,"

"I can stay. I'm on vacation, not due back to work until next week."

"So, you'll stay?"

David whispered, "Yes, for you I will."

David had the nurse bring in a cot, blanket, and pillow. She also gave Denise her medication, so she could sleep better. David watched her as she nodded off to sleep. She was so beautiful, he hated to see her in the position she was in. An abusive relationship—she didn't deserve that. How could this happen to her? David wanted to do so much for her; he wanted to protect her, but would she allow him to do it? He'd take care of her.

They were both successful. Success only helps take care of a person financially. He wanted to care of her with all his heart, to take care of the emotional part. She needed that, and he was going to be the man to give it to her. She wouldn't have to want for anything. He loved her independence; that was a true turn-on for him. David thought about many things until he closed his eyes and drifted off.

David awakened to a scream. It was Denise. He jumped up and asked, "What's wrong?"

Denise replied, "It's my leg." She kept shaking her leg.

David, in a panic, "What's wrong?"

Denise started crying. David yelled for the nurse. David said, "Denise, what's wrong, what's wrong?"

Denise said, "My leg, my leg."

"I know—what's wrong with it?"

Denise replied. "It's itching, and I can't get to it."

David started laughing. Denise couldn't see the humor in it. She had a cast on above her knee. David looked for something sturdy and thin enough to get to that area. He took a wire hanger, carefully snaked it down her leg. David asked, "Where does it itch?" She grabbed his hand. Her hands were soft and warm. She moved it to where the agonizing itch was. She took a deep breath and said, "Thank you, that feels so much better."

David looked into those big brown eyes. They sparkled like stars. He gazed at her and she gazed at him the same way. They were interrupted when the nurse came in. She said, "Is everything okay?"

Denise said, "Yes, I'm okay now." She held David's hand when she responded to the nurse. A warm feeling came over David. That gazing session they were having—hopefully, that would happen again. Denise had been in the hospital for about a week. David visited her every day, she was improving daily.

Dr. Peterson knocked on the door, said, "Good morning, young lady. I see that you are getting better and better. Your arm and leg will be in a cast for about six more weeks. Other than that, you are free to go home. I have some prescriptions for you. One for pain; it's a low dosage, and the other is for prenatal vitamins." David looked up like he had just seen a ghost. Denise must've seen the same ghost because she had that same look David had.

Denise said, "Who's pregnant?"

Dr. Peterson said, "You are! That's why I gave you a low dosage for the pain pills, so it won't hurt your baby. You didn't know?"

Denise said, "Apparently not."

Doctor Peterson replied, "Yes, young lady, you are five weeks pregnant." He handed Denise the scripts and said, "It looks like you need some time to process this; I'll give you your privacy." Doctor Peterson left the room. Denise looked out the window with this blank stare. David was speechless. He didn't know what to say.

She turned to David and said, "Thank you for coming. I appreciate all that you've done for me." She rang for the nurse.

David responded, "That's it?"

"Is that it what, David?"

"You're just going to end it like this?"

"End what, David? End what? What do you want from me. I'm a mess."

"Not to me you're not."

Denise said, "I'm banged up and broken, not only physically but emotionally."

David replied, "You will heal."

"I'm being stalked and threatened by my ex-boyfriend, and I'm pregnant with his baby. Don't even know if I want to keep it."

David replied, "You're keeping that baby."

"My plans were not to raise a baby by myself."

"And you won't."

The nurse walked in. Denise said to her, "Dr. Peterson said that I can go home. Can I check out now?"

"Did he give you your prescriptions?"

Denise replied, "Yes, he did."

"I'll go and get you a wheelchair then."

The room was silent. Neither David nor Denise said anything. David started to bag up Denise's belongings. David said, "I'll drive you home." She agreed and turned her head toward the window. The nurse came back with the wheelchair. David helped Denise out of bed and into it. David gathered up all her items, and they headed towards the elevator.

David heard Denise crying. When they got in, he knelt by her and wiped her tears. He asked, "What's wrong?"

Denise replied, "All these years I wanted you, and this accident brought us together. It's like a Love Collision."

David replied, "In a way it was. I didn't expect us to meet like this."

David drove Denise home. Helped her up the stairs to her bedroom. He took care of her. Weeks went by. She finally got the casts off her arm and leg. The baby bump was starting to show. She decided to keep the baby. Her ex-boyfriend was arrested for trespassing after he stalked her when they were coming from the store. Charges were pressed; that was one less thing she had to worry about. David went with Denise to all her doctor visits.

David helped with the nursery. He gave Denise a beautiful baby shower; when it was time for the baby to be born, he was right there in the room with her. She birthed a baby girl, with eyes just like her mother's, and she named her Destinee. David signed the birth certificate as the father. They planned on getting married. This Love Collision brought them to their Destiny (Destinee).

HEART OF GOLD

An angel in disguise—you just never know when you'll meet one. Lincoln Ave is the street Nina walked down when she got off the bus. She worked from three to eleven; it was always quiet that time of night, and she knew the neighborhood. She never worried about anything. She lived four blocks down the street, so the walk was not that long. In her routine walk, she always saw a certain homeless man; it seemed like he was always at the corner of the block waiting for her.

He never asked Nina for anything, but she'd always offer him something. There were times when she saw him, times when she didn't. When she did, she had a conversation with him. He always walked her to her house. She thought that was kind of special. She felt he was her protector. When she approached him, Nina said, "Hello, Jordan." She called him Jordan; he wore Jays from back in the day.

Jordan responded, "Hello, Nina. How are you?"

She replied, "I'm good."

"Shall we walk?" He said, "I've been waiting on you, how was your day at work?

"It was fine." Nina worked at a nursing home. She loved the people there. Sometimes she stayed past her shift, just to make sure they were tucked in and had what they needed. They were her little children. She looked after five patients but checked on ten. Nina asked Jordan, "Where have you been?"

"On cold nights, I check into a shelter. They let you come in for twenty-four hours. In the morning, you have to leave and make room for someone else; it's a rotation routine, so I try to find something from day to day." Nina thought, *that's a rough road to be going down.* She felt sorry for him. Just when she thought that, he said, "Oh, don't feel sorry for me. I thank the Lord for every day I wake up. I still have my limbs and my health; I'm going to be just fine." Wow, she loved his faith talk. Nina thought, *if he's fine, then I'm fine.* She got to her doorstep and handed Jordan a sandwich and ten dollars.

She said, "Okay, Jordan, we'll do this again tomorrow?"

He responded, "Looking forward to it." He waited until she got in the house, then he was off to enjoy his sandwich. Nina thought about him that night. She said a prayer for him. Some people have a special place in her heart, and Jordan was one of them. Saturday was a no-work day for Nina, so she cleaned the house; she was cleaning out some drawers of old clothes and came across some old sweatpants and shirts. She thought about Jordan.

Nina did a load of laundry and put in a double dose of fabric softener, so his clothes would have that fresh smell. As soon as they dried, she put them in a bag, walked down the street where she knew to find him. She heard screaming before she got around the corner. Two men were beating him up.

"Help, somebody! Leave him alone, help, help, somebody," Nina screamed. One of the men took his sneakers, kicked him in his chest and left. She hurried up to Jordan. His mouth was bleeding. She knelt to him, and said, "Are you okay?"

"No, I'm hurting."

Nina called the police. The ambulance arrived and took him to the hospital. Nina rode along, telling him he was going to be fine. She wasn't sure, but she hoped. She prayed for him. At the hospital, they got him to a room. He had two fractured ribs, a concussion, and he needed five stitches in his lip, but he would recover. They kept him overnight, and she stayed to make sure he would be okay.

Jordan was forty. He had lost everything to a fire some years ago, he told her; he had no family here, so he had been moving from place to place for some time. Nina had met him a year ago coming out of the store. The plastic bag that had her groceries in it broke. Jordan was sitting on the curb, and he came right to her rescue. He found a new bag, gathered up the oranges and coffee and cheese and chicken and put them in the bag. He'd been around ever since.

The nurse came in to check on Jordan and said he could leave in the morning. Nina thought, *leave and go where? He's bruised up.* She thought about her guest room. Did she want him staying with her? She knew him, but did she know him well enough to stay in her house? Nina quickly prayed that night. She didn't want him on the street bruised, but could she trust him in the house?

She already knew the answer but was waiting on the Lord to give her a no—nope, that wasn't happening. Nina already knew he was going to be staying with her. She asked Jordan, "How are you feeling?"

"I'm in pain, but I'm blessed because I'm still alive." Nina was amazed at his response; he was a true man of faith.

"Do you have somewhere to go?" She felt convicted in her spirit; she already knew the answer to that question.

He said, "I can find somewhere to go."

Nina replied, "You already have a place to go; you're coming to stay with me."

"I can't impose on you like that."

"You're not."

He said, "Are you sure?"

"Yes, I am sure."

Jordan was released from the hospital. They caught a cab home, and he struggled to get out of the car; he was banged up pretty good. Nina helped him out. She paid the cab fare, helped him up the stairs, unlocked the door, and they went inside. He went straight to the couch.

"Are you okay?" Nina asked.

"I will be." Nina didn't mind Jordan on her couch; he was homeless, not dirty. She'd never seen him dirty; he always maintained his looks. He was scruffy but not dingy, but he did need a razor. She left that decision up to him. Nina asked him was he hungry.

"I could eat." She ordered pizza and wings. The guest room was upstairs. He wasn't up for climbing so he slept on the couch. They watched movies that night; she had a bathroom on the first floor, so it was easier for him to use that one.

Jordan said, "You have a nice place."

"Thank you."

"How long have you lived here?" Jordan asked.

"Two years."

"Are you renting, or do you have a mortgage?"

Nina replied, "I'm renting for now. I'm single. I don't really want that burden on me right now I like where I'm at."

He replied, "You ought to think about it."

"Maybe one day." Jordan was good company for Nina. He could hold a conversation; she was seeing another side of him. She thought, she saw homeless people before, but he just didn't seem like the others. Maybe it was his faith that made him different. Nina told Jordan, she was heading to bed.

"Have a blessed sleep and night."

"You do the same." All night she thought about how he couldn't stay in her house while she was at work. Would he steal? Would he invite people in? All these thoughts went through her head. *Peace be still* was what she heard in her spirit; she shut down every negative thought and off to sleep she went.

Morning came. Nina smelled something—was that breakfast? She put on her robe, went downstairs. She didn't see Jordan on the couch. She walked into the kitchen and saw all these pots on the stove, pancakes, scrambled eggs, coffee brewing, sausage sizzling.

Jordan said, "Good morning, Nina!"

She replied, "Good morning, Jordan. What is this?"

"You are taking good care of me, so I wanted to return the favor and cook you a nice breakfast."

"You can cook?"

"There are a lot of things I can do. Have a seat, Nina; I'll make your plate." She sat down, he made her a plate. Every bite she took melted in her mouth. From the pancake to the coffee, it was a delish delight.

Nina asked, "How are you feeling? Are you doing any better?"

Jordan said he was getting better; he felt a little stronger. He managed to go outside and get the newspaper. Going down was easy, coming up was a struggle. Each day he got stronger. It put a smile on Nina's face; his words bolstered her faith. "I won't trouble you any longer. I'm getting back to my old self. I have a shelter I can go to; I'll leave out with you today on your way to work."

Nina thought she couldn't let him leave until he was totally healed. She said, "No, you can't go. Who will cook me breakfast in the morning?" Jordan smiled; Nina did too. She was starting to feel like the Good Samaritan, but she wasn't looking for a reward. She remembered the scripture, *Your Father, who sees what's done in secret, will reward you openly.* She didn't tell her co-workers or friends that Jordan was staying with her; she kept that between God, Jordan, and herself.

Two o'clock, it was time to go to work. Nina was on her way out the door. Jordan said, "Can I walk you to the bus stop?"

"You don't have any shoes!"

Jordan said, "But I still have feet. Shoes never stopped me from walking, they just cover my feet."

Nina responded, "You don't let anything stop you from doing what needs to be done."

"Not today, or tomorrow. If it's the Lord's will, I will do it." He opened the door, and off they walked to the bus stop. He stood with Nina until she got on the bus. He nodded his head when she got to her seat; the bus pulled off, and he walked back to the house.

Nina's shift at work was a lot of fun. Her children, (the elderly) were a bundle of joy. She was happy when she spent time with them. She read to them, helped them get dressed, combed their hair, watched TV with them. They made her day go by fast. She felt like she was taking care of them in her home, instead of working. She loved them.

Around 10:45 pm, Nina checked on them. She went in every room to see what they were doing. Some were reading, others watching TV or sleeping. Her routine check for the night was a wrap; she clocked out and prepared herself for the forty-five-minute ride home. The bus pulled up to her stop, and there was Jordan waiting. Nina stepped off the bus and said to Jordan, "How was your day?"

He said, "Normal. Do you know how to drive?"

"Yes."

He asked, "Do you have a license?"

"No."

"Maybe you should get one."

She replied, "For what? I don't have a car."

"It's still good to have a license. Then one day if you decide to get a car, you will already have what you need to drive it. Plus, you're working these hours—you shouldn't be catching the bus this late all the time."

Nina said, "I never thought much of it. I have enough expenses, with rent and bills. I can barely keep money in my savings and checking accounts; I don't need an extra bill."

Jordan replied, "It's just a driver's license. That's not a bill, right?"

She replied, "Yeah, you're right." She then asked, "What are you going to do once you get better?"

Jordan replied, "I am better."

"That's awesome." They went in the house; the aroma smelled amazing. "Jordan, what did you cook this time?"

"Just a pot of soup."

"That's not soup I smell."

Jordan said, "Well, what does it smell like?"

"It's a lot of different aromas."

"Well, all that can't be in a pot of soup?"

She replied, "It could be." He took the lid off the pot, and everything she smelled was in the pot: oxtails, collard greens, tomatoes, green beans, carrots, potatoes, onions, garlic—you name it, it was in there.

Jordan put some in a bowl, gave her some crackers, and poured her a hot cup of tea. She took a spoonful of soup. It was heaven on a spoon, and it nourished her body. "How did you learn how to cook like this?" Nina asked.

Jordan replied, "I just do it." He taught himself; whatever he felt like doing, he did. Nina felt warm and fuzzy after that. Jordan cleaned up the kitchen. Nina said goodnight to him and headed upstairs. As she opened her bedroom door, she looked down; there was a driver's license study book. She didn't question it; she knew it came from Jordan. Nina studied it like she was cramming for a surprise exam. Tomorrow was Monday; she didn't have to go to work, so it was an all-night study.

Jordan knocked on the door. Nina said come in.

Jordan said, "Are you ready to take a pop quiz?"

Nina replied, "Sure!" Jordan asked her questions, and she missed one; he asked her the questions again until she got them all right.

"Are you ready to go take the test?"

"I think so."

Jordan replied. "Let's go!"

Nina said, "Before we go anywhere, I'm going to buy you some shoes."

"Does my bare feet bother you?"

She replied, "No, but you have to have something on your feet to go in certain places." He nodded.

"I can't afford to buy you a pair of Jordan's, but I will buy you a nice pair."

"Whatever you buy me, I'll appreciate it." At the shoe store, he looked around and saw some Nikes. He tried them on and was happy with them and so was Nina. Off to the DMV they went. She took the test and passed it on her first try. She got her picture taken. Nina was so happy she got her license. Jordan looked at her like a proud daddy.

Jordan said, "Now you need a car!"

Nina said, "WHOA! I don't need another expense."

Jordan replied, "What makes you think it's your expense?" He always said something that encouraged Nina, but what he just said was so over the top. Nina said no more after that.

"Come with me. I want to take you somewhere."

Nina replied, "Okay." They went downtown to a car dealership. They walked in and were greeted by two salesmen. They said hello to Jordan and he responded. "Hello."

Nina looked at Jordan. "You know them?" Jordan nodded.

He said, "Have a seat; I'll be right back." Nina sat down, looked around, and saw this Black Charger, black and sleek. It had a big red bow on it. She could see herself in that one; it was beautiful.

She walked over to get a closer look at it. Tinted windows, sunroof, all the bells and whistles. The black was lacquer; it looked like it was waxed with the best products on the planet. The tires and rims made that car stand out. There wasn't a price tag on it, but she loved this car. She slid her finger across it as she walked by, then she looked at the bow. It had something written on it. She walked up closer to read it. It said, JUST FOR YOU, NINA. PAID IN FULL.

Nina put her hand over her mouth with excitement. She turned around and there was Jordan, with the whole sales team. Jordan looked different; he looked brand new. He had shaved, had on shirt and slacks; he was dressed to the nines. He said to Nina, "Thank you for all you've done for me and my family."

Nina said, "Family! What do you mean, family?"

Jordan said, "First off, do you like the car?"

"Like it? I love it!"

Jordan replied, "I knew you would." He then said, "We have a couple of places to go, and then I will tell you everything. Are you ready to start her up?"

"Yes!"

Jordan said, "First, let's go back to your house; I have something to show you." They drove back to Nina's house. He said, "Come upstairs, I want to show you something." They went upstairs to the guest bedroom. Jordan opened the closet door and turned on the light. Nina could see markings on the wall: year, age, and names, Jason, John and Sam.

64

Nina asked, "What is this?"

Jordan replied, "This house you live in is the house I grew up in; my name is Jason. The markings on the wall are a height ruler. My brothers and I would measure each other every month to see who would be the tallest. We did it in this closet, so our parents wouldn't see it; it's been here for decades." Nina was speechless.

"Those gentlemen you saw at the dealership are my brothers John and Sam; before I say anything else, we have one more place to go."

Nina said, "I don't know if I can take any more surprises. Before we go anywhere else, I need to go to my job and pick up some paperwork."

Jordan replied, "That's fine; that was the next place we were going."

"Hmmm," Nina said. They drove to her job. Nina said, "Hello, everyone."

They responded, "Hello, Nina." Then they turned to Jordan and said hello to him, adding, "Your mother is expecting you!"

Nina said, "Your mother? Where?"

Jordan said, "Let's walk, I'll show you." They walked down the hall, into the room, and Jordan said, "Hello, Mom!"

"Hey, baby, how are you?"

"I'm fine."

Mom looked at Nina and said, "Hello, Sunshine."

Nina replied, "Hello, Doll." Nina had taken a liking to her years ago and now she loved her very dearly.

Mom said to Jordan, "Did she like the car?"

"Yes, Mom, she loved it."

Nina asked, "What's going on?"

Jordan replied, "My family owns multiple businesses. We do a PAID IN FULL BLESSING every year, and each year one of us picks a candidate. This year was my mom's turn, and she chose you. My mom told me about you; she said you have a Heart of Gold. I had to see for myself. Here's comes the ironic part—when I met you last year it was my turn to choose a candidate. When your groceries fell out of your bag, and I came to assist you, I wanted to see your reaction. You didn't treat me like I was homeless. You had a caring heart; you fed me; you checked on me. Mommy, she even went to the hospital with me."

Mom said, "Hospital!!! When???"

Jordan said, "I'll tell you about that later, but she took me in, and she made sure that I was taken care of. She didn't leave me out in the street bruised up. You were right, Mom, she does have a Heart of Gold, and for that, Nina, you'll receive a double blessing." Nina looked astonished.

She said, "What do you mean, double? The car isn't a double blessing."

Jason said, "No, the car is one blessing; the house is another. My mom bought the car for you; I'm giving you the house. Nina, you are now a homeowner." Jordan handed Nina an envelope with the deed to the house, along with money.

Nina said, "What is the money for?"

Jordan responded, "That is all the rent you paid last year. Every time you sent your rent, we'd put it in the bank. We never kept your money. Now you can start a savings account.

"Again, I say thank you for taking care of my family. You do have a Heart of Gold, and it is very pure."

Nina gave Jordan and his mom the biggest hug ever. Nina said, "I was just being who I am."

Jordan said, "And this is why you are being rewarded for being who you are...."

SURPRISE

"Looking at my Gucci, it's about that time." The concert was over, and Liz was on call to pick someone up to take to Trenton, New Jersey. Why did she pick this fare? Liz was writing her first book. She had been saving money. To pick up extra cash, she did Uber on the weekend. This fare was for $150; that was the amount she needed to put her at $2000, for editing, publishing, and book covering. She'd been working on her book for some time. She wanted to publish it before year end. As she was waiting, she got a text from Keith, her boyfriend.

Keith asked, "Hey, baby, what are you doing?"

"Waiting on a fare. What are you up to?"

"Lying here thinking about my baby."

She said, "Which one?"

Keith replied, "Stop playing, you know you're my baby."

Liz replied, "Just checking."

Liz and Keith had been dating for about seven months. They lived two hours away from each other. They'd been managing; they were committed, but Liz found it hard not seeing Keith all the time. Although they were distant, she trusted him. Keith never came off to her as the cheating type. They talked and texted as often as they could. Liz received another text for another fare. The fee went from $150 to $300 because there was another person riding to the same destination. Liz was excited; it put her over the top. She would put that extra money toward buying her ISBN codes.

She saw the two ladies, and she waved to them. They got in. Liz said hello and gave them her name. They introduced themselves.

"Hello, my name is Gina, and this is my best friend Patrice."

Patrice barked out, "I can speak for myself. Hello, Liz, my name's Patrice."

They all laughed.

Liz said, "It's nice meeting you ladies. Are you ready to ride?"

"Yes."

Liz asked, "You mind if I turn on some music?"

Patrice responded, "No, that will be fine."

Liz turned on some vibe music, and off to Trenton they went. The trip was an hour and forty-five-minute drive. Liz didn't mind; the fare was already paid for. Besides, she drove that far to see Keith. This was business, pleasure would have to wait. It was a smooth ride, no traffic at 10:00 pm. They made it there at exactly the time her GPS said she would.

The address they gave was a hotel. Liz thought, *oh, they are having that kind of night.* Patrice gave Liz a $50 tip. "I love the vibe of your music. Thank you for putting me in a good mood."

Liz said, "You're quite welcome."

Gina said, "Good night, Liz."

"Good night, ladies."

As Liz was driving off, she noticed a certain vehicle in the lot. It looked very familiar. She texted Keith to see what he was doing.

He texted back, "Hey, love, I'm in bed asleep. What's up?"

Liz said, "Oh nothing, just wanted to see if you were still thinking about me."

Keith responded, "You know I am."

Liz drove off. Before heading back, she decided to get something to eat, then gas up. After getting a bite to eat, she pulled up to the gas station. It had started raining. She put on her hoodie jacket and ran inside to pay for the gas. Of all days she left her debit card in her jeans at home. As she was walking back to her car, she noticed that the same car that she seen at the hotel was at the pump. She slowly walked to her car, glancing over. OMG, it was Keith! Liz took a quicker look. He was with Gina, the lady she had just dropped off at the hotel.

Liz didn't want to cause a scene. She got in her car, glad she didn't drive her own car; he would've noticed it. When she did long distance drives, she borrowed her roommate's car. She texted him, "Hey, baby, me and the girls are thinking about riding into Trenton tonight. Let's get together. I'll be there about midnight."

He texted back, "Baby, that would be great, but I have my son this weekend. We will make plans."

Plan what, Liz said to herself; she had heard that for so long. She texted back, "FINE." Keith knew something was wrong. He said, "Why did you say it like that?"

Liz didn't respond. She sped off. She wasn't in the mood to argue; she just wanted to get home, plus she had just made $350, so she had enough to keep her occupied when she got home. The rest of the weekend, she had fares locally, which kept Keith off her mind. Sunday, as the day wound down, Liz received a text from Keith.

He said, "What's up, baby?"

Liz replied, "Nothing, what's going on with you? How was your weekend with your son?"

"It was good."

In her mind, she said, I bet it was.

He texted, "Next Friday I'd like to take you out for breakfast."

Liz replied, "That will be fine."

The work week was the same; it went by quickly. On Fridays, Liz didn't take fares until the evening. Breakfast with Keith was convenient for her. He swung by and picked her up. Keith said, "I miss you, baby!"

That was new; Liz never heard that one before.

She replied, "I miss you too. So, when are we going to spend some time together since you miss me so much?"

Keith replied, "I'll keep you posted."

What does that mean? Liz thought, but she wasn't in the mood to ask questions. Keith always left Liz in a loop; she didn't feel like she was in a relationship. At times, she wanted to change her status from, "In a relationship" to "Run like hell, this is too complicated!" They got to the diner and ordered.

Keith said, "What's wrong, Liz? You look like you have something on your mind."

"I'm fine."

"You use that word quite frequently!"

"Oh, you've noticed!"

Keith replied in a soft whisper, "I notice everything about you."

That was new. Keith never showed concern before. She didn't want to ask why the sudden change. Did he really care about how she felt? She was too burnt out to ask. Keith was never much for conversation, and now he wanted to talk? She was exhausted! Since he wanted to talk, she let him do just that and she listened. After breakfast, Keith wanted to go to the mall. Liz had time to spare; her fares didn't start for another five hours. Keith knew Liz did Uber, but he didn't know when she did them in his area.

They got to the mall, did some window shopping. Keith had an appointment at Men's Warehouse to get fitted for a tuxedo; he was going to be the best man at his friend's wedding. David's Bridals was on the other side. They made it one store, two businesses, a brilliant idea—the bride and groom could get fitted at the same time. While Keith was getting fitted, Liz sat down and glanced at this gown in David's Bridal. It was the most beautiful gown she had ever seen. She walked over to get a closer look.

She felt the material; it was silk. The saleslady came over. She looked familiar to Liz. She couldn't put her finger on it, but she knew she'd seen her somewhere before.

She said, "Hello, my name is Patrice, can l assist you?"

Liz thought, *Patrice, Patrice, that ride to Trenton, could this be the same lady?* She responded, "No, I was just looking at how beautiful this gown was."

Patrice replied, "My friend is getting married. This is her gown. She was coming into town this weekend, but her plans changed. I need to get her fitted. You are the same height and you're built the same way; can I use you as a model for her fitting?"

Liz said, "I don't mind, but my boyfriend will be out soon."

Patrice said, "It won't take that long."

"Okay."

Patrice started taking the measurements and wrote down the information. She said, "I'd like to see how long the gown will be on her. Can you try it on for me, so I can see if I need to hem it?"

Liz said, "Sure." She carefully put the gown on. It was the most beautiful garment she had ever had next to her skin.

Patrice asked, "If you were choosing a shoe for this dress, which one would it be?"

Liz picked out a pair of satin heels. The gown was perfect. Patrice didn't have to hem the gown; it hit the floor just right. Liz turned around to look in the mirror. She loved what she saw; she felt like a princess. The gown looked like it was made for her. It fit her curves to a perfect T. She was in awe with the vision; she felt so beautiful. Whoever was going to be wearing this gown would wear it well. Liz said to herself, *I will make a beautiful bride one day.*

Patrice said she had all the information she needed. Liz stepped down off the pedestal, changed her clothes and handed her the gown. Patrice gave Liz a I'm-so-happy-for-you kind of smile. She thanked Liz for being her model.

"It was my pleasure."

Perfect timing! Keith was finished getting fitted, and he said, "Are you ready to go?"

Liz said she was.

She thought about the gown during the ride back to her place. She didn't tell Keith about it, but she wished she had taken a picture in it.

When they got to Liz's place, Keith said, "Your birthday is coming up soon. I'd like to take you on a cruise; can you see if you can get some time off?"

Liz said sure. He told her the dates and gave her a gentle kiss on the cheek. It was soft and gentle, like an I love you was attached to it. Liz was feeling something for Keith, but she wouldn't tell him. She smiled and said she'd text him later. Buzz, buzz, her phone went off. Time to Uber. All fares this weekend were local, which was good; she didn't feel like doing long distance drives. Sunday night, Liz wound down. She poured a glass of wine, grabbed her book and started writing. She got a text from Keith. It said, "We won't be able to meet at the same hotel, we'll find a different one, can't wait to see you."

Liz said, Oh, two can play that game. Ten minutes later, she texted back. "I had such a good time with you last night. I think I left my earring in your bed."

Keith called. She didn't answer. He called her eight times that night; she didn't pick up. All his calls went to voicemail. He had disturbed her mood, and he'd have to suffer; she wasn't picking up or returning calls. Whatever he had to say, it could wait; she wasn't hearing it tonight. Early Monday morning, she got a text from Keith. "Good morning, Beautiful, we need to talk." She ignored it.

She got ready for work, stopping to get an iced coffee. She arrived at work and put in her request for vacation. She didn't feel like a cruise, or being with Keith, but she put in for it anyway. Every year she took off for her birthday. Another text from Keith came through. "Are you just going to ignore me?"

Guess so. Liz was not responding. The work week went by fast. She had been working on her book and that made time go by faster. When Liz worked on her book, she thought less about Keith.

Thursday, the day before she went on vacation, she got an edible arrangement delivered to her job. It was from Keith. The note read, "You are so special to me in so many ways. I hope you have a wonderful birthday." He never made her feel that way, but those were his words. She didn't text him to say thank you. To her, nothing felt sentimental, so she shared her fruit with her co-workers.

Clocked off from work, she went home, got into her jammies, turned on some jazz, grabbed her book and started working on her bio. She turned her phone off. She didn't feel like doing Uber tonight; she wanted to be alone. That's how she felt with Keith—in a relationship but still alone. It sucked. She wanted to send him a text to say this is not working, let's just be friends, but her heart was saying hold onto him. She erased the message, kissed his picture goodnight, and off to sleep she went.

Friday was finally here. *"Happy birthday to me,"* Liz said, in a blah mood. She didn't feel like celebrating; she didn't feel special or loved. She got dressed, put on a pair of white jeans and a striped tee, and treated herself. She got her nails, pedicure, and eye wax done, and picked up a smoothie. She turned on the Uber app at 3:00 pm, no fares. She went to the park to gather her thoughts, wrote in her book for a little bit. Around 3:45pm, she got a fare to, of all places, Trenton, NJ. She didn't have time to go pick up her roommate's car. She gassed up hers and drove to the destination to pick up her customer.

The gentleman got in the car and smiled at Liz like he knew her. He gave her the address, and the long journey began. Liz turned off the app; she didn't want another fare, especially since she was driving long distance.

The gentleman asked, "How are you?"

Liz said, "I'm fine."

He asked, "What's your name?"

Liz replied, "None of!"

"None of?"

"Yes, None of your business!"

He laughed. He said, "My name is Michael."

"Nice to meet you, Michael, my name is Liz."

Michael said, "This isn't another joke, is it?"

"No, that's my real name."

Michael said, "I'm pleased to meet you."

"Likewise."

"What are you up to today?"

Liz replied, "It's my birthday. No plans."

Michael said, "A beautiful lady like yourself doesn't have any plans? Your man isn't taking you out anywhere?"

"No and because of that I don't feel like celebrating."

"I know you don't know me very well, but I'm going to a party. If you're not busy, maybe you'd like to join me."

"What type of party is it?"

"It's a birthday party."

Liz thought *how ironic. Why not; I'm not doing anything.* The fare was $175; that would take care of her for rest of the day. She liked being in Trenton, so she said she'd think about it. They got into Trenton at a good time.

Michael said, "We're early; it's only 6:00 pm. The party doesn't start until 7:30; how about we stop and get something to drink?"

"Okay."

They went into the mall and stopped by Starbucks; she got her favorite iced coffee. They sat down to talk. Liz liked to talk with her hands, and her hand hit her coffee. *Splash*. The coffee spilled all over her white pants; she was so embarrassed.

Michael asked, "Are you okay?"

"Yes, it's just white pants. I need to change. I can't go anywhere looking like this."

Michael agreed. They stopped at a store and Liz found a cute halter dress. She tried it on and liked it. Michael said, "Let me see it on you." She came out and he said, "You wear it well." She smiled, and he asked, "Where's the price tag?" She handed it to him.

A few minutes later, he came back with a bag for her other clothes. Michael said, "Happy Birthday, Liz."

Liz replied, "Thank you, Michael."

Liz looked at her watch; it was 7:15pm. She said, "It's time to go."

Michael replied that he was just thinking the same thing.

They got on the road. It was a twenty-minute drive. They pull up to the house. It was kind of dark, but there were a lot of cars outside. They went to the door and it was unlocked. Liz was hesitant about going in, but Michael said, "Don't be scared." He went in first. Liz stood on the outside, and Michael came out to get her. He said, "It's okay," and Liz slowly walked in.

Liz said, "What kind of—"

Before she could get the rest of her words out—

"*SURPRISE*"!

Liz was speechless. She saw all her friends. Keith spun her around and kissed her. He said, "Happy Birthday, Beautiful! Marry me, Liz! Will you marry me? I wanted to marry you the very first time I saw you, Liz. I knew it was too soon, but in my heart, I knew you were my wife."

Liz stunned said, "I never picked that up in your behavior; I always felt I was on the outside looking in."

Keith said that he knew he was bad at showing his emotions, but in his heart, he knew Liz was the one. "Let's get married; let's do it next week."

Liz said, "Wait a minute. I didn't say yes."

Keith said, "You didn't have to, your eyes said it for you." He slipped a two-carat ring on her finger. She held her hand out, admiring it. She loved it.

Then Liz said, "We can't get married so soon; I don't have a gown." The bedroom door opened and out walked Patrice from David's bridal and the young lady who was in Keith's car that night.

Keith said, "Liz, I'd like for you to meet my sister, Gina; she flew into town for this occasion. This is her best friend, Patrice."

Patrice said, "The day you came into David's Bridal, Keith made an appointment for you to get fitted for your gown. Keith and Michael were in the other room watching the entire time. Keith

79

shed tears. He saw how beautiful you were in your gown; he picked that gown for you."

Liz turned to Keith. "You did all this for me?"

Keith said, "All for you, baby!"

Liz said, "I remember the night I dropped Patrice and Gina off at the hotel, I was so confused. I saw your car there, Keith. When I texted you, you said you were home, then I saw you at the gas station with Gina. I thought you were cheating on me. When I texted you again, you said you were home. Before we walk down any aisle, explain that text I received that night about meeting at the hotel."

Keith said, "That text was for Patrice. She's a wedding planner. I texted her about meeting somewhere else. The hotel I was going to book the party at, the Banquet Hall, flooded, and I had to find another place to have it. Since it was getting close to your birthday, I had to find another place quick. I didn't want to have it at my place; it would ruin the surprise, so I had it here at Michael's place. I'm sorry I lied to you, but it was all a surprise. I didn't even know you were in the area."

Liz said, "So that's what that text was about?"

Keith said, "Yes, now let's talk about the text you sent back to me!"

"I thought you were cheating on me. I knew you didn't mean to send that to me, and I thought I'd give you a taste of what I was feeling, but I didn't do anything. I've been faithful to you."

"And I to you."

Keith kissed Liz. The party was awesome; it turned out to be a birthday and engagement party. They left for the cruise the next day. Even though Liz had her gown and shoes, she decided to wait, and they planned their wedding for the following summer. Liz published her book and dedicated it to Keith. She still is on cloud nine about her birthday party; it was the best surprise ever. Keith went all out just for Liz, and she loves her some him.

TAILOR MADE JUST FOR ME

"And then there was light." The pool lights automatically came on at 7:00 pm. Megan had seen them come on from her kitchen. She knew what time it was when they came on; she set the timer specifically for that time. It was her wind down time to gather her thoughts for the day. After washing the dishes, she'd pour herself a glass of wine, walk out to the patio to sit by the pool, close her eyes and listen to the waterfall. It sounded soothing and peaceful. She muted that sound and listened to the beat of her heart. It sounded hurt and painful; it almost sounded like it needed to be resuscitated.

Her heart had been drugged through all the seasons. Now it was cold and frozen like winter—the look she gave people matched how she felt. Megan would give men a cold chilly look that would break them if they looked at her long enough. She wouldn't let anyone get close to her; she'd shut down quicker than a dirty diner. She'd been rejected by some, hurt by many. She couldn't fault the men she'd had in her life; she'd positioned herself to be treated that way.

She lowered her standards to be a doormat for them. Megan had more footprints on her body than the ones in the sand. She trusted no one. If you tried to get close to her, she would put up her porcupine defense; you'd feel the pinch from her needles. Megan wasn't always this way; when she loved, she loved hard. Her heart was created to be that way, but it had been broken so many times, she decided to turn it off, be frigid, and offer men the wrath of her cold heart. She needed to love herself, love herself as deeply as she loved them. She didn't think about relationships for a while. She needed time to herself to heal, evaluate who she was.

She took a deep breath and reached for her glass. *CRASH*! The wine glass hit the ground. "*GREAT*," a perfect crystal wine glass destroyed. She looked down at the glass—that was her heart. *Shattered to pieces*. Broken. She was a mess. She never gave herself time to heal, so every relationship she was in, she would love with slivers of her heart, not with her whole heart. She was missing herself. She couldn't completely love anyone. If her heart were whole, she would've loved herself first. She chose not to, and now she was shattered and scattered.

Megan went in the house to get the broom and dustpan. When she returned to sweep up the glass, she glanced up. She saw a falling star and couldn't take her eyes off it. It almost looked like it was coming towards her, like that star was just for her. *Do we wish on stars anymore?* Megan wondered. She followed it until she couldn't see it any longer. Whatever happened when she saw that star, she went from feeling chaotic and cold to calm and warm. She shook it off. Whatever she didn't shake off, she took to bed with her that night.

She slept through the night—no heart palpitations, no night sweats, no disturbing dreams. Megan slept so well, she overslept.

She jumped in the shower, put on something quick, and out the door to her car she went. She didn't have time to get breakfast, so she grabbed a Danish in the cafeteria. She ran to the elevator, pushed the button, and the doors opened. She hit the button for the 12th floor. As the door was closing, she saw a hand pushing the door back. A gentleman stepped on. Their eyes meet. His eyes pierced her soul. No words were spoken. She had never had that feeling before, from any man. He investigated her soul, and her whole body felt it. She shook for a minute.

Who was this man? She had never seen him before. Why did he make her feel this way? The door closed, and he grabbed his phone to answer a call. Megan looked at the numbers on the elevator going up. For some odd reason she felt comfortable with him, although they hadn't spoken only made eye contact. He made her feel safe. He ended his call, and she reached her floor. The door opened, and he hand-gestured "ladies first." Megan walked off, heading towards her office. She glanced back at the elevator to see where he was heading. She saw him standing against the wall, looking straight at her. Her body shook again. *What in the world was going on?* She was to find out in a matter of days.

Megan walked into her office and to the window. She sat in her chair to look outside. The sun rays hit her face, and she closed her eyes. All she could see were his eyes. The blaze from the sun made his eyes so vivid. They were staring into hers. His eyes were peaceful. She didn't know if it was the warmth from the sun or his eyes, but something was making her melt. There was a knock at the door. Megan said, "Come in."

Renee, her secretary, came in with flowers. "These were just delivered for you."

"From whom?"

Renee said, "I don't know, the delivery service just dropped them off. There's a card inside."

She opened the card. It said, "You were Created and Tailor made just for me," no signed name or anything. The roses were beautiful. They were carefully handpicked. She loved the vase they came in too. This was no ordinary glass vase. It was unique, hand-crafted. The colors were vibrant. She sat at the edge of her desk, admiring the beauty of what just arrived. Her phone rang; there was a meeting in ten minutes. She had forgotten she had a conference call. She grabbed her laptop and onto the meeting she went.

As she was walking down the hall, she passed the elevator. The door was closing. There he was. Their eyes met again. His eyes were drawing her to him. By the time she approached the door, it had closed. Megan touched the door softly and sighed. She looked at her watch. She had five minutes to get to the meeting. Walking quickly, she looked back to see if he was there. Not a soul in sight. She sighed again. What was happening? What was so different about him? Who was he? Where did he come from?

During the conference call, Megan was thinking of his eyes. They had her lifted into a hypnotic state; what kind of encounter would it be the next time they saw each other? Would she see him again? She twirled her pencil during the meeting. If they had asked her questions, she would've failed miserably. Her mind was elsewhere. She didn't want to be at work; she couldn't concentrate on anything. After the meeting was over, she told Renee to cancel all other meetings. She could do that; it was her company. If anyone really needed her, they could call her cellphone. She left her flowers at work. They looked so beautiful on her mahogany desk. Her hands were full—laptop, purse, blueprints, no room for flowers.

With her hands full, she could barely hit the button for the elevator. It was crowded this time. She looked around to see if he was here. No, not on this ride. She felt that was not going to be her last time. He had left an impression with her, in her soul, and it was a good one. She walked to her car. There was a card on her window. The card read:

"I hope you like the roses; they were handpicked just for you. Every rose I picked, I thought of you. The different colors define you. The white one is for purity; you love with a pure heart. The yellow one is your sunshine; you brighten the day. The red one is for your heart; when it is healed and made whole, you can love again. I made the vase with my hands, intricately. I took my time molding and making it. The colors I picked to paint the vase; I thought of your beauty and your smile. The vase is uniquely made, just like you are. The scripture came to mind, *I am the Potter, you are the clay.* As I set the clay on the wheel, I thought of how God was putting you together just for me. Some of the roses' stems were thorny, but your heart is a rose. The thorny stems are your protection around your heart. I need you to do me a favor. I need you to remove the thorns around your heart, so I can love you, so that you can love me. Sincerely, Anthony."

Megan needed an usher from church to catch her; she was about to faint. Her knees buckled. She held onto her car, so she wouldn't fall; she wobbled a little, but she managed to get in. She couldn't drive. She sat in her car for twenty minutes, her body shaking. *Why does my body react to him like that? Could it be him?* The one who sent her the flowers, the gentleman she saw in the elevator? It had to be him; her body didn't have this reaction until she saw him. Even the card he wrote made her body react. She couldn't believe what was happening; this was powerful. Although she was in a daze, she started her car and drove home.

Megan was so mesmerized when she got home, she almost took a shower with her clothes on. She fixed something to eat, then lay across the bed, staring at the ceiling. She was starting to feel complete; she felt loved. She felt his arms holding her, and she felt safe in his arms. She dozed off into a peaceful sleep. At midnight, she woke up to go get a drink of water. She walked to the kitchen and thought of the falling star that night. She remembered how she felt afterwards—this is extraordinary and powerful. As she went to the refrigerator, she noticed something shining on the patio floor.

She walked out to the patio to get a closer look. It was a sliver of glass from the night before. She tried to pick it up, and it pricked her finger. It was a little hole, just enough to draw blood. It felt like a paper cut. She rinsed it off, put a Band-Aid on it, went back to sleep. "Alexa, what time is it?"

"The time is 7:30 am."

Megan lay there feeling the throb from her finger. The bandage was too tight. She took it off, but it was still bleeding. That was odd. She wrapped it up again, got dressed for work, headed out, stopped in the cafeteria, had breakfast, finished up, walked to the elevator, got in, pressed for her floor, and stepped back with her back against the wall, door closing.

Suddenly, there he was, Anthony. He walked up to Megan, put his hand on her back, put his other hand on her chest. He looked at her with this fire in his eyes. He looked deep into her soul. She felt her heart mending; she felt fire all through her body; she felt like she was going to faint, but he held her up. She began to melt. She was no longer frozen. He just stared at her with fire in his eyes. Tears were running down her face, like they were racing each other. She couldn't take her eyes off his, and she couldn't speak; she could only look at him. He then kissed her with a passion unknown, his lips soft and tender, breath as fresh as a mint. She couldn't resist him. After the kiss, he stepped back. He touched her face; his hands were warm and gentle.

He began to say, "You were broken for so long, Megan; you were breaking your heart more by not healing. I couldn't let you die."

Megan said, "Die? What do you mean let me die?"

88

Anthony said, "I had to come save you, from you before you let someone break your heart, where you would die. Megan, you were meant to love me and only me. I had to come find you fast, mend you back together." He then showed her his bandaged finger. He grabbed hers. It was the same finger, the wedding finger. He took his bandage off, hers too. Both fingers were still bleeding. He took his finger and pressed it up against hers. When he pulled them away, immediately, the fingers stopped bleeding.

Anthony said he pricked his finger from picking the roses. He couldn't show Megan who he was until she pricked hers. He said, "I had a dream last night to meet you here at this appointed time, to stop this blood flow so our hearts can start to beat as one. The night of the falling star—remember that? I know you saw it too—I didn't know if I was wishing or praying, but this fire burned within me. There was something extraordinary about it. When I saw you in the elevator, Megan, I knew you were mine. My body shook. Something leaped in me. That had never happened before. I loved you before I even knew you. I was carrying you in my spirit for some time now. I knew there was going to be someone unique for me. You were always unique in the way you loved; no one could understand you. Your love is a different language. Only I can understand the rhythm and beat of your heart. Your heart is just like mine. I was made strong enough to carry you. You were broken, and I needed you to heal. I needed you to complete the beat in my heart. For that to happen, you had to be made whole. Do you understand what I'm saying to you?"

Megan said, "Yes, I do. No one understood me. My love has languages that are not easily translated."

Anthony said, "Other than God, I am the only one who will understand you, Megan; you were *Tailor made just for me*. Let me show you and love you for a lifetime."

NAKED TRUTH

Staring in the mirror, Geneva was trying to find the right hairstyle to wear. She was precise about how she looked. She had flaws, but only she knew them. She didn't date anyone because she was embarrassed about certain things about herself she couldn't change. She didn't want anyone judging her, so she stayed to herself so that she wouldn't have to show who she really was. She wasn't a bad person; she just wasn't good at being transparent to others.

She fed her dog Shadow, her best friend. She could be herself around him. He didn't judge her; he loved her regardless. She kissed the tip of his nose goodbye and out the door she went. Geneva was currently going to school for culinary arts; she loved to cook. She wanted to become a chef one day and own her own restaurant. She did catering jobs on the side, so she was already building her clientele. They loved her food, so that was a plus for her.

Today in class she had to take a test. She had to know certain food, food prepping, and food temperatures. She had been studying all week for this, and she was ready for it. If it was a pop quiz, she still would've been ready. The test was an hour and a half. She had ninety questions to answer, and she was done in forty-five minutes. She handed her test to her teacher, Mark. While he was waiting for the others to finish, he graded her paper. He had an astonished look on his face.

He walked over to Geneva and handed her the paper. She smiled, and so did Mark.

He asked, "How did you know all the answers?"

Geneva replied, "Cooking is my passion. Since I don't do anything else, I just study."

"What do you mean you don't anything else?"

"I don't have a life after I leave school."

"Why not?"

"I'd rather not say." The timer to end the test went off.

Mark said, "Okay, you guys, turn in your papers."

Class was over; Geneva grabbed her purse and was getting ready to leave. Mark said, "Geneva, I'd like to have a word with you." She shrugged her shoulders and sat back down. Mark waited for the students to leave. He pulled up a seat next to her and asked, "Why don't you have a life? You're a beautiful girl with a lot going on. I see you don't smile a lot. The first time I saw you smile was when I gave you your test results."

Geneva replied, "I didn't know you were looking at me."

"I look at all my students, but you are the unique one."

"What do you mean?"

"You stand out. You're mysterious. You're a loner but not lonely. You give so much of yourself, but no one understands you. You talk with your eyes; you listen with your heart." Geneva couldn't believe someone understood her. She knew she was different, but why did he take notice and no one else?

Mark said, "The night is still young; can I take you out to dinner?" Geneva was anxious to know what else he had to say.

"Sure, I would like that."

"I want you to trust me."

"Why?"

He replied, "I need you to." She thought that seemed kind of odd. What did he need her to trust him for? They walked across the street to the restaurant. Mark opened the door for Geneva, and they were seated at a table.

Mark asked, "Would you like a glass of wine or something?"

Geneva replied, "Merlot would be fine."

Mark continued the conversation where he left off. "Geneva, you have flaws that you don't want to share, but how would someone know who you are if don't open up?"

She replied, "I plan on being by myself for the rest of my life."

"Why would you do that? The world needs you."

"What world?"

"My world. You are my world, and I am yours. You have a love that I need. That's why you're so closed up. You haven't been appreciated. You have a rhythm of love, and it has levels. Your love is like a choir, tenor, alto, and soprano; it starts low, and eventually it will take me higher. Since I've been talking to you, you have been opening up your heart to me; you understand what

I'm saying." Geneva nodded. "I've seen you smile more in an hour than I have in the last three months. Do I have your attention?"

She replied, "Undivided."

Mark said, "I couldn't let you go another day without me telling you this. I am a gentleman; I am going to take my time with you. I don't want anything from you; I just want you to know you don't have to be alone. I understand you, Geneva, because I am you. You are my mirror; I see myself in you. You are not to be taken for granted. You are that diamond that no one has seen before. There are so many facets in you. You're like buried treasure. Someone would have to dig deep to find you. You are a jewel that has not been seen in a crown yet; you were hidden just for me, and now that I've found you, I want to take care of you."

Geneva couldn't believe what she was hearing. She said, "All this time you were there. Why didn't you say anything?"

Mark replied. "You weren't ready."

"Ready for what?"

Mark replied, "Me. You weren't ready to open up to me three months ago. It's time for you to change, change your look, change the way you think about yourself. I noticed you always wear scarves and wigs; why is that?"

"I'd rather not say," Geneva replied.

"Open up, Geneva, talk to me," Mark asked. She liked the sound of his voice when he pleaded with her.

She replied, "I cover up my head because I have alopecia."

"Alo who?"

"It's called alopecia. It's a skin disease that attacks the hair. It falls out and doesn't grow back. I have patches of hair missing from my scalp."

Mark replied, "I've never heard of that before."

"Well, I have; it's been like that for years."

"I'm sorry to hear that, but doesn't it feel good to open up?"

"Yes, it does."

"Are you ready to order?"

"No, I like to just talk if you don't mind," Geneva said.

"You're not hungry?"

"This conversation has taken my appetite."

Mark smiled and said, "Never heard that before."

"I don't want to waste food or your money," Geneva replied.

"Well then, would you like another glass of merlot?"

"If you don't mind."

"For you, I'd buy the whole winery."

Geneva replied, "Now I'm really drunk."

"The only way to be drunk is in love." They both smiled.

Geneva asked, "Where have you been?"

"What do you mean?"

She said, "I've wanted someone like you for so long. I've been in relationships that were so shallow, and I thought something was wrong with me."

Mark replied, "We are deep people, Geneva; deep calls out to the deep. We probably weren't ready for each other. Certain things needed to mature in us; when it was time for me to appreciate you, that's when I found you."

"Do you think you have?" Geneva asked.

Mark replied, "I believe so. The words that I've told you didn't come out of me until tonight. I'm forty years old. If they were to come out with someone else, it would have a long time ago."

Geneva said, "That's very interesting."

Mark said, "And I am very interested in you."

Geneva replied. "Oh, so did I pass my test, or did you curve grade me on the sly?"

"No, you passed your test, I believe in doing things decently and in order. You have the knowledge to be a chef. I want to be honest with you. If I did your grading on the sly, I would not have been honest with you or myself." Geneva loved the way that sounded. She was getting comfortable with Mark; she felt she didn't need to protect her heart any longer.

Geneva said, "Maybe one day you could come over, and I can cook dinner for you?"

"I would like that."

"I have a dog that is very territorial."

Mark replied, "That's fine; I like dogs." Mark paid for the drinks, and they headed out. Mark said, "Can I drop you off to your car?"

"I don't have a car."

"Well, can I take you home then?"

Geneva smiled and said, "I would like that." On the ride home, Geneva asked, "So what was your life like growing up?"

Mark replied, "I was a nerdy kid. I was always in the books, never went outside much. I was a loner much like yourself. I didn't click with everyone. All through my life I was like that. I was a circle to squares, so I never fit in anywhere. Life was enjoyable. I knew what I was supposed to do, that's why I never married. I knew my wife was going to be cut from the same cloth as me, so I kept my body pure for her. I had relationships, don't get me wrong, but I had a thirst, and you are the water to quench it. I couldn't drink from every fountain, but what you have for me, Geneva, will be satisfying." Geneva was speechless.

They pulled up to her place. Geneva said, "Dinner at 7:00 pm tomorrow?"

Mark replied, "I won't be late." Mark walked Geneva to her door and waited until she made it inside. As he walked back to his car, he felt a pain in his chest. He thought it was heartburn and didn't worry. He got in his car and drove home.

The next day Geneva went to the store to pick up some items for dinner. Leg of lamb was her specialty; Mark would like that. She felt this awkward feeling in her spirit, something unusual like an alert. She texted Mark to see what he was up to. He texted back, "picking up a bottle of merlot." She texted, "Good, it will go great with the leg of lamb." He responded, "Can't wait to taste it." She sent him a smiley face. When she got home, she started cooking. It was about 3:00pm. She wanted to make sure everything was just right.

Mark texted her around 6:00 pm. "You mind if I come early?"

Geneva responded, "No, not at all." There was a knock at the door. She looked through the peephole; it was Mark. She opened the door, saying, "Oh, you were right at the door. You surprised me!"

Mark responded, "Yes, for some reason I felt the need to come early."

"That's fine; are you ready to eat?"

"No, but what I need you to do is undress for me."

"Wait a minute."

Mark replied, "I apologize, no disrespect to you, Geneva, let me say it in a better way so you understand what I'm saying. I want the naked truth; I want to see your hair."

Geneva was hesitant. "Why do you need to see it?"

He said, "I want to know more about you, all of you. Do you trust me, Geneva?"

"I do trust you, Mark."

He replied, "Let me see who you really are." Mark sat on the couch, put a pillow on the floor. He said, "If you don't mind can you sit on floor in front of me." She trusted him, so she sat on the floor between his legs. He took off her wig, and she began to cry. He said, "Don't cry. I promise I will not judge you." He took off the braided cap that was under it. She had spots of hair missing on her scalp. He said, "It's okay, Geneva, it's just you and me."

He started taking her braids down. She cried more. He said, "Baby, it's okay." He took all her braids down. There was one spot in her head that was not from alopecia, and he asked what that was.

She responded, "I had a head injury many years ago as a child. The pressure was so heavy, they had to drill in my head to take the pressure off, and that spot never grew back."

Mark said, "Geneva, turn around so I can see you." She turned around; she had her head down. He put his hand on her chin and lifted her head. He said, "You are so beautiful."

She responded, "I don't feel like it."

"If you looked in the mirror now, you wouldn't think you're beautiful? What my eyes see, you don't feel, because I see you for who you are. I am the only one that will ever see you like this. Trust me, Geneva, be yourself for me. The naked truth is I get to see you without you being covered up. I would like to wash your hair."

She said, "Now?"

"Right this minute! I want to be a part of the process."

"What process?"

"I'm going to love you so much your hair will grow back; I want you to feel my love in my fingers on your scalp."

She said, "OMG."

"Yes, you'll say that too when you see the results. Go get the shampoo and towel." He started the water, rinsed her hair, poured shampoo, and slowly massaged her scalp for five minutes. She felt her scalp tingling. He rinsed, put conditioner on it, let it sit for two minutes, and rinsed it. He said, "Go blow dry your hair; I'll be waiting for you on the couch." She dried her hair and returned to the living room where he was waiting. Mark said, "I want to massage your scalp before I braid it."

Geneva said, "Okay." He massaged her scalp with coconut oil. Geneva felt relaxed; she was enjoying every minute of this therapy. He braided her hair back up; she grabbed her scarf and wrapped her hair up. Mark asked, "Now how do you feel?"

"I feel free."

He replied, "And you shall remain that way." Suddenly, Mark grabbed his chest and fell on the floor.

Geneva said, "Mark, what's wrong? Mark!" She laid him on his back; he was having a heart attack; he wasn't breathing. She had taken CPR classes, so she knew what to do. She called 911 and began to do CPR. She said, "Mark stay with me, stay with me." She did CPR until the ambulance arrived. They rushed him to the hospital. Geneva was right with him. He needed emergency surgery; he had a blocked artery. He was in surgery for hours.

They put a stent in him. Surgery was a success, and they moved him to the ICU to recover. Geneva stayed with him. He was still under sedation, and she needed to be with him. She felt connected to Mark, and she couldn't leave him now. When his eyes opened, she wanted to be the first person he saw.

Nurses came through the night checking on his vitals, changing out the IV bags. Geneva was the watchman on the wall; she slept, but when she heard someone come in; she was wide awake. She wanted to see everything they were doing to Mark. When they left, she walked over to his bed, stroked his forehead, and whispered in his ear, "You wake up for me, Mark, I need you to love me." Morning arrived, the doctor walked in and motioned for Geneva to come to the door. She walked over.

The doctor asked, "Are you his wife?"

"I would love for her to be." Geneva turned around; Mark's eyes were slightly opened but she heard his voice.

"Baby, how do you feel?"

He said, "I feel better now that you called me baby."

Geneva smiled. The doctor said, "As I was saying to Geneva, if she had not done CPR on you right away, you would have been brain dead by the time you got to the hospital. She kept oxygen in you long enough. Her quick performance saved your life."

Geneva replied, "OMG, you came to the house early for a reason. What if you were in your car driving and this happened?"

Mark replied, "I know, there was a reason I came early. Thank you for being there for me, Geneva; you saved my life."

"Thank you for coming into mine and helping me open my heart to you; looks like we both had open heart surgery." They laughed.

Mark said, "You are in mine forever."

Geneva replied, "I believe you will be in mine that way also."

To Be Continued

101

A COVERED LIE

"Wake up, sleepy head," Geneva said as she pulled the curtains back. She was waking Mark up, so he could eat his breakfast and take his medicine. He had been put on a strict diet, and she was making sure he stuck to it. It had been two weeks since Mark had a heart attack, and he was glad to be home. Geneva wanted to keep a close eye on him, so he was staying at her place. He had stairs at his house, and she didn't want him climbing them until he was strong enough. Her apartment had everything on one floor, so it was easy for him to get to everywhere, and she took a leave from school.

Geneva gave up her bed; she slept on the couch. Shadow, her dog, got used to Mark being there, so Shadow slept in the bed with him. Geneva said to Mark, "Do you want to eat breakfast in the kitchen or I can bring it to you?"

Mark replied, "I can eat in the kitchen." Shadow jumped down off the bed and followed Mark into the kitchen; he sat on the floor next to Mark.

Geneva said, "I'm a bit jealous."

Mark replied, "Why?"

"My dog doesn't know me anymore."

Mark said, "Well, I guess I'm part of the family now."

Geneva smiled. "How are you feeling?"

"It's strange, Geneva, but I don't know how I feel. I never thought I would have a heart attack. When something like that happens to you, you don't know how to react to it. The reality is I had a heart attack, but what's in my mind is why did it happen to me. So, I'm still processing that event."

Geneva replied, "I can relate and understand what you're saying."

Mark replied, "Can you?"

"You have no idea." She then asked him was he ready to eat, and he said yes. She made him scrambled eggs whites with turkey bacon and wheat toast with orange juice. Shadow was looking at Mark like, *I'm hungry too.*

Geneva said to Shadow, "Go eat your food; leave Mark alone." Shadow looked at Mark with those puppy eyes. Mark gave Shadow a piece of turkey bacon. Shadow swallowed it like water, not taking time to taste it, and wanted more. Geneva said, "I see why he likes you; you've been giving him treats on the low."

Mark said, "Prove it."

Geneva said, "It's a hung jury; I have no evidence."

Mark replied, "Case has been thrown out. Meeting adjourned. Want another treat, Shadow?" They laughed.

Mark said, "I want to thank you."

Geneva said, "What for, may I ask?"

"For taking good care of me, opening up your home to me, making me feel better."

"You started it."

Mark replied, "Started what?"

"You started making me better. I'm starting to think different, feel different about myself. I'm starting to feel comfortable around you."

"I'm glad you're starting to be yourself," he said.

"It feels so good, Mark."

"And it should."

"So, what would you like to do today?"

"Let's take a walk in the park," Mark replied. "Strap Shadow up with his leash and let him run wild while we stroll and talk."

Geneva said, "It's a good day for a stroll."

"Let's put it in motion then."

Geneva cleaned up the kitchen. Mark put Shadow's leash on, and to the park they went. Shadow was running, pulling Mark. He wasn't quite ready for that yet, so he took the leash off and let him run.

"Geneva, tell me about your childhood."

"I come from a single-parent home. My life wasn't always great, but I learned to forgive my abuser. My mother was my abuser; I still have scars. But it didn't make me bitter. I never knew why she did it. I was too young to understand. As I got older, I would run away. I didn't want to be found, and when she did find me, the beatings were worse. Mark, I don't want to talk about this anymore."

Mark said, "Okay, honey." As they walked, Mark grabbed Geneva's hand. He knew she needed comforting; he could feel her pain. He wanted to let her know that he cared; not about what she shared but how she felt afterwards. Mark couldn't do anything about her past but was going to make her future happy and secured.

Geneva asked Mark, "How does it feel walking? Do you feel a strain on your heart?"

Mark said, "No, I feel fine; I needed this fresh air." Geneva smiled. He said, "You want to sit down under this tree?"

"Sure." They sat down; Mark sat up against the tree, Geneva laid her head in his lap, looking up at him. Mark said, "How did you know I wanted you to do that?"

She replied, "I just knew. Your heart sends signals."

"What else does my heart say?"

Geneva closed her eyes. Mark caressed her face. Geneva said, "Your heart says, *let me rescue you, Geneva, from your pain. Trust me with your heart. Don't run away from me, run to me.*" Geneva opened her eyes with a tear streaming. "Was I right?" she asked.

Mark wiped her tear. "So right," he said. "So, so right, baby."

Shadow came back, pounced on Geneva and licked her face. Geneva laughed. "Well, I guess that's our cue to head back home."

Mark said, "I enjoyed this moment with you."

"It was much needed," Geneva replied. Mark put the leash back on Shadow and headed back home.

When they get home, Mark said, "Geneva, it's time to get your hair washed again."

She said, "I know. I've been so busy with you I don't bother with me."

"Never forget about yourself. Always take care of you. I'll make sure you do that." Geneva took her scarf off and took her braids down. Mark shampooed her hair, put a hot oil treatment in, washed it, towel-dried it, massaged it with oil, and braided it; he did that routine every weekend. Geneva didn't have to do her hair; Mark was her personal beautician. He loved Geneva, and anything he could do to help her, he did.

She was a giver as well. They poured into each other, nothing lacking. The same measure he poured into Geneva, she poured back into him. They never outdid one another; they were balanced. They found out more about each other by being there for one another. They were each other's strength; where he was weak, she made him strong. The less he did for himself, the more she did for him; the less she did for herself, the more he did for her.

They knew what each other needed, and they were not selfish with themselves; they gave freely to each other in an unconditional way. They were one and didn't know it yet. Well, Mark knew; Geneva was getting ready to know.

Geneva asked Mark, "What do you want for dinner?"

He said, "Something light."

"Okay, let me take a shower and after that, I'll fix dinner."

"Okay."

Geneva went to take a shower. Mark was playing with Shadow. Mark heard Geneva scream, and he jumped up and ran in the bathroom. "What's wrong?"

"I stubbed my toe on the tub, ouch, ouch, ouch."

Mark said, "Oh, I thought it was—"

"It was what, Mark?" Geneva asked. He just stared at her.

She said, "What's wrong?"

He said, "Your breasts!"

Geneva forgot she didn't have her towel on. She quickly picked it up, wrapped herself up, and turned around.

Mark said, "Geneva, turn around."

"No."

"Please turn around for me, Geneva. Please," Mark said. He walked up to her and slowly turned her around. He opened the towel, and she started crying.

Mark said, "Don't cry, baby." Geneva had no breasts, just scars. "What happened?" Mark asked.

"They lied to me, Mark; they lied to me."

"Who lied to you, Geneva?" Mark replied.

"I went for my yearly mammogram. They found lumps in both breasts. They wanted to look a little further. They didn't say anything to me about removing them; they just wanted to do a biopsy. I went under anesthesia, and when I woke up, both my breasts were gone. They were gone, Mark; they were gone." She started crying again. "That's why I wanted to be by myself for the rest of my life. Who wants a half of a woman?"

Mark held Geneva as she cried in his arms.

"Why would anyone want me, Mark?"

"I want you."

"Why! I have nothing to give you."

Mark replied, "Because your breasts are gone, Geneva, you can't love me? Your breasts are gone, not your heart and your emotions. Geneva, look at me, look at me, baby; tell me right now you don't love me. Look at me please; tell me you don't love me."

Geneva said, "I do love you so much, Mark."

He replied, "You are all woman. There are women who have breasts who can't come close to who you are. You are genuine, baby; the more flaws you have, the more beautiful you become." Mark touched her scars, then he gently rubbed them. "I'm going to love all of you. If you had breasts, it wouldn't have mattered to me. I love you because of who you are, not what you can give me.

"No matter how many flaws you have, Geneva, I won't stop loving you. You're so pure. I've never known anyone like you before, and I know there is no one else out there like you. You're not missing anything to me—you have everything I need. If I can accept this, so can you. Be free, Geneva, be free, baby. You are whole. Although you have that part of you missing, you are still whole. Believe in yourself. I do."

Geneva said, "I love you so much, Mark. I carried this weight all these years because I thought I would be laughed at, rejected, but you showed me that there is a real man who can love me."

Mark said, "I am the only man that's going to love you." He kissed her on the cheek. He said, "Is your toe okay now?"

Geneva said, "Everything is okay."

He said, "Now take your shower, and let me get back to Shadow. You know he gets jealous if I leave him alone too long." A month later, Geneva went back to school. Mark went back to teaching class and they both came back stronger. Geneva's hair was growing back so beautifully; she was no longer wearing scarves and wigs, her skin was glowing, and she was smiling more. The hidden gem was now shining.

She graduated two months later. A year later Mark and Geneva got married. They had their wedding in Mark's backyard. Shadow was the ring bearer. He was doing fine coming down the aisle until he saw a squirrel—good thing the best man had the rings. Geneva planned on opening a restaurant—her dream—with the help of her husband. Happy and secured, they lived together, all four of them: Mark, Geneva, Shadow, and the baby on the way.

CAN I TOUCH YOU THERE?

Eleven fifty-nine: in five, four, three, two, one, on the air red light comes on. "Good evening, midnight lovers; welcome to my radio show, *Essence of Intimacy*. I'm your host, Desire, I am new to the radio but not to the facts that I'm about to lay on the tracks for you tonight; this will be a no-call show. I have a flight to catch, and I wanted you to hear my voice tonight.

"This show will be recorded. If you would like a copy, I will gladly send you one free of charge. That is my gift to you. I want to talk to you on a deeper level of intimacy. 'Can I touch you there?' is the topic. This is for mature audiences only, an audience that understands what it is to love someone from the inside. The beauty of a person always comes from within. Outside beauty fades; inside is eternal. The best story to tell is your own, so let me share mine with you.

"His name is Kendrick. I met him on impulse. I was getting on the train, and he was coming off; we both turned around as the doors were closing; we both put our hands on the window of the door. His eyes were inviting. I felt a magnetic connection with him. I wanted to open the doors and jump off. I knew that couldn't happen. He kept his hand on the door until the train moved. His eyes never left mine; they were focused on me like we were saying our last goodbye, but it was our beginning.

"Every day like clockwork, I would arrive at the subway station at the same time, to see if I would see him. I didn't. I wanted to. I wanted to see his eyes again; they had a message for me. Weeks and weeks had gone by. At times I would pace the platform, waiting for his presence. I thought, could he be searching for me, like I am for him? Why does that scripture come to me— when a man finds a wife, he finds a good thing? Was I supposed to be looking for him?

"I finally called off the search. My train was coming. Should I wait for another one or get on this one? I walked slowly to the train and got on, sat down and looked out the window to see if he would come down the stairs. Nothing. I turned my head and closed my eyes for the ride home. The train shook on the tracks, and it caused me to open my eyes. I saw a man wearing a black fedora. He had his head down. I couldn't see his face, and he had what looked like a sketchpad; he was drawing something.

"I closed my eyes again. I had four more stops to go. The stations were ten to fifteen minutes apart. Before I got to the next stop, I opened my eyes. The man in the black fedora was standing by the door with his back to me. I didn't think anything of it. The stop came, he got off, I looked out the window, and there he was. The man in the black fedora was Kendrick. I smiled; he looked at me and tilted his hat to me; he then began to walk up the stairs. Did he know who I was? Why didn't he say anything?

"The train began to move. Would I see him again? Just as so many thoughts went through my mind, a young lady walked up to me and said, 'The gentleman told me to give you this when the train started moving.'

"She handed me this paper, it was a drawing of me with my eyes closed. At the bottom of the picture it said, 'A part of you has not been touched yet. Can I touch you there? Sincerely, Kendrick.' I thought *what part of me hasn't been touched yet?* He left an address for us to meet on Saturday. I finally got to my stop. At home, I kept thinking, *what part of me hasn't been touched yet? How did he know about that?*

"Saturday came. I was skeptical about meeting him. I checked out the place online. It was very elegant, pricey, nothing under fifty dollars. I stopped by the place during the week to see the activity. It was always crowded. I was relieved; there would people around us. As I walked in, I was escorted right away to my seat; a bottle of Moet on ice was waiting for me. The waiter poured a glass for me; he lit the candles on the table.

"I sipped the champagne. Suddenly the lights went out, and all the candles from the tables lit up the room. All I heard was ooooh. Everyone in the room sounded like a choir in harmony—then silence. I looked around. All eyes were on me. I heard footsteps coming towards me. Kendrick approached the table, took my hand and said, 'Follow me.'

"We walked towards the patio. Waiters came and slid open the doors for everyone to see what was about to take place. Two seats

112

on the patio were waiting there for us. He sat me first. Kendrick nodded his head to the waiter. Gold glitter started falling, and it was snowflakes.

"Kendrick sat down, and he said, 'When I saw you on the train, we were strangers. When we passed each other, you became my soul-mate. I gravitated to you. That's why our hands were on the window; you felt the same thing. Desire, you were destined to be my wife before the foundation of the world was made. All the years of my youth I knew who you were. I desired a certain type of woman. I began to search for you; I prayed and fasted for you, and I yearned and craved for you. You're in love with me.'

"I said, 'How do you know that?'

"Kendrick replied, 'Love is like a butterfly. Your heart was in formation as a caterpillar; it was wrapped up in a cocoon real tight. You were saving it for someone special who would love you the way you wanted to be loved. A certain feeling unknown to you would overtake you, one you've never felt before. You'll have no control over it. When it's time for you to love, your caterpillar (heart) that was in formation will turn into your butterfly. That is vital information that you need.'

"I asked, 'Why is it vital to me?'

"Kendrick replied, 'Because you need to know why you're feeling what you are now.'

"I said, 'I don't feel anything.' Kendrick took his hand and put it on my throat and then my stomach. I gasped and closed my eyes.

"He said, 'What do you feel now?'

"I responded, 'I feel a quiver, like double heartbeats.'

"Kendrick said, 'That's what I felt when you walked past me. I knew I had to find you. I was out of town for business for a couple of weeks, but I knew if that's where I saw you, that's where I'll find you again. I memorized the scent of your perfume and knew if I smelled it again, that would be you. That night you got on the train, I smelled that familiar scent. It was an aroma revelation that you were near. I moved closer to see if it was you, and it was. Your eyes were closed. I saw the beauty of your spirit. You were so innocent looking, almost angelic. I said to myself there she is, my wife, she's beautiful when she sleeps.

"'I couldn't wait to kiss your lips, your skin looked smooth, like silk. I wanted to hold you, and do so many things to you, but my focus was to touch your soul. Can I touch you there?'

"I whispered, 'Yes, please.'

"Kendrick got on his knees and spread apart my legs gently. His head leaned into my stomach, his hands caressed my back. He looked up into my eyes. His eyes had words of passion written on them. He said:

As deep as the ocean is the depth of your soul,
The fire that burns within you can melt any coal,
There's a certain desire in you that only I can quench,
My spiritual eye is required to see and maintain the element,
You are beautifully created, a woman full of grace,
You were kept hidden until the right time and place,

I was going to find you and it would be very soon,
To see my heart's desire under this beautiful moon
Please don't you worry I only have eyes for you.
You will become my wife Desire after you say I do.

"Kendrick took my left hand he kissed the tips of my fingers. He did something unique with my ring finger—he stuck my whole finger in his mouth and seductively slid it out. He put a ring of promise on it, and then said, 'I promise to love and protect you, minister and guide you, bless and caress you, adore and explore you. Desire, you deserve the world, and I'm here to give it you. I'll love you today, tomorrow, and until the end of time, say yes to me, Desire.'

"I replied, 'I don't know if I could love you the way you love me.'

"Kendrick said, 'Trust me; you will.'

"'Then I say yes to you.' Everyone in the restaurant stood up and applauded. I couldn't believe what I did. Kendrick promised me the world, and I said yes to it. Did I know him that well to have a future with him? How stable was he? All my questions went away within a month's time. I never had anyone love me the way he does. Everything he promised me, he gave, and then some. I never knew a man like him existed.

"His voice is so melodic; when he sings to me he drenches my soul; it feels like a poetic rainstorm. I want to say this to you, midnight married lovers out there. Put God first in your marriage.

Love every piece of your spouse, to the core of his soul, her soul; love them unconditionally. If you have an argument, apologize quickly. Never go to bed upset. Make up loving is fun; do it quickly and passionately.

"Teach and learn something new, surprise, arouse, play, have fun, and date your husband/wife. Be their best friend. With all that being done, you'll be able to grow old together in harmony and joy.

"Soon to come to your newsstand is my sister Simone's magazine, *Beautiful Lover*; I know you will enjoy her articles.

"My time is up. As I told you I have a flight to catch. Kendrick and I are celebrating our tenth wedding anniversary in the Bahamas. He is my king, and I am his queen. Everything I told you to do in your marriage, we are doing in ours. My name is Desire, thank you for listening to my radio show *Essence of Intimacy*, peace and love to you all......Goodnight."

INTIMACY

Please allow me to slip into something a little more
comfortable
Something like your mind
I'm stimulated by your kind
Because your thought processes excite me
Deep and Wet with the waters of critical analytical thinking
Flowing like the rivers of time
Can I gently caress your intellect?
With concepts that I have created with mine
As I undress your thoughts with my eyes
I know what you want because imagination never lies
The truth is all in your head I know because so
Am I
It's better that way
Wetter that way
Because these creative juices never stop flowing
All the while knowing
What I wanted you gave me a piece of your information
Must be intimidation that has you seemingly nervous must be
your first time
Sharing your mind
Don't worry, it won't hurt

But you might get addicted

Because once you get the feeling it's hard to stop no longer

being restricted

By physical limitations having inclinations to do it

Every time I see you

Not in public though,

Someone might see

But they still wouldn't know

The places we would go

How I softly licked your gray matter

As we rolled around your brain's master

Bedroom trying not to knock anything over

I know you never felt like this you never had it this deep

You feel exhaustingly weak

As if you were asleep

But it wasn't a dream; it's truly real just without the ability to

feel

In fact, we hadn't even kissed, and yet you miss

Me slowly thrusting my swollen creativity,

Deep inside your imagination rhythmically,

Until our thoughts exploded simultaneously

We just engaged in mental intercourse

BEAUTIFUL LOVER

"Simone, Simone, did you see him?" Robin said as she ran into Simone's office.

Simone replied, "See who?" Robin grabbed Simone's hand and pulled her like there was a fire and they needed to get out quickly. "Girl calm down, what's going on?" Simone said, Robin still pulling her, and they stopped.

Robin said, "Look!" Simone looked with this OMG look, she then walked back to her office, plopped down in disappointment. "What's wrong?" Robin asked.

Simone said, "If you're looking at him like that, so is every other woman in this department. Yes, he's fine and all, but believe me, he's either married or dating someone, and he's serious about her. I'm not wasting my time or eyes on him; you guys have fun." Next thing you know, ten women surrounded the office. Simone looked at Robin and said, "I told you, you wouldn't be the only one looking at him. Now let me get back to work while you hens go clucking over that rooster."

Robin said, "But he's so fine."

Simone replied, "And he knows that too. You ladies are just boosting his ego. Go get some work done, Robin." Simone got up and went over to the office where the ladies were and said, "Ladies, I pay you to work, not twerk. We have to be on schedule;

we have a deadline to meet for the new edition, snap, snap, chop, chop." Simone was the CEO of *Beautiful Lover*, a magazine company. She had started the company three years ago, around the same time her sister Desire's radio show, *Essence of Intimacy,* first aired.

Simone's spirituality was deeper than Desire's. Simone came up with the name of her company when she saw the perfect man. She saw beyond the color of his skin. She had never called a man "beautiful" until she saw him. She pitched the name to Desire; Desire asked her husband Kendrick about it. He liked it, so did Desire, and so did Simone, so *Beautiful Lover* became the name of her magazine. It had been successful. There were articles about love, soul searching, pictures of people, clothing, cities, and foods. She liked to show the beauty in all creation, but the origin of her magazine's name was the beauty of the person.

Simone was meeting her sister and brother-in-law for dinner later that evening. They were coming back from celebrating their wedding anniversary. She also had a meeting with the gentleman in the office. Simone called to make sure the reservation was set for tonight, locked up her office and headed to the other office for the meeting. She walked in and the gentleman said, "Hello, Simone."

Simone replied, "Hello, Beautiful Lover." Yes, the man the women were going crazy over—Simone knew exactly who he was. She used to date him years ago. His name was Jesse. She was in love with him, still is. When she first saw Jesse, it was at a class

120

for new business owners; he was a teacher and financier for small business owners. Wealth was in every inch of this man; it was in his knowledge. Simone fell in love with his mind.

He taught from a level of profound understanding. Although it seemed like owning a business would be difficult, it sounded perfectly easy coming from his mouth, and she was all over his, white teeth, moist lips—. She liked the shape of them when he spoke. When he smiled, the dimples in his cheeks looked like drilled holes, they were so deep, and that's how her love for him was. He loved her but wasn't in love with her. At the time he was seeing Simone, he was also seeing someone else. It wasn't serious at the time, so Simone and Jesse dated for a while.

Until one day Jesse said he was getting married. Simone's heart broke. She couldn't believe what he had said. Although she told him how she felt, it didn't change his mind. She didn't date anyone after that, didn't want to go down that road again. She used all her energy, time and passion to build her business; that became her love, and that's where she remained to this day.

Jesse asked, "How have you been?"

Simone replied, "I've been fine and yourself?"

He said, "All is well. I came by to see how your business was doing, if you needed any pointers to make it better?"

Simone replied, "No, everything is going well."

Jesse replied, "That's good. I also came to tell you your loan is paid off."

Simone replied, "I thought I had four more years to go?"

He replied, "Our company looks at small businesses when they start out; we look at the progression, and when the business looks promising and prosperous, we invest in it. When the stock goes up, we put some of the profits toward your loan. I don't do that for everyone, but I did it for you. I believed in your vision; I saw how passionate you were. You had so much faith in it, and prosperity was written all over you. I knew if I invested in your company, it wouldn't be a disappointment. Your revenue is awesome. People are buying your magazines; your sales have tripled. Simone, you have a good fan base; keep up the good work. Tonight, celebrate your continued success."

Simone replied, "I will do just that."

Jesse said, "I'm glad you came to my class; you are a few of many."

Simone asked, "What does that mean?"

Jesse replied, "Many start out, few succeed. Congratulations on your vision. I'll see myself out." He opened the door, and women were standing there like groupies. Jesse said, "Ladies." They parted the hallway like the Red Sea.

After he got on the elevator, the women ran into the office where Simone was sitting, asking all kinds of questions.

"Is he married? Does he have children? Does he need a mistress? Is his bathwater in bottles?"

Simone replied, "Ladies, ladies, ladies, did we meet our deadline?" They sighed and went back to work. Simone thought about the meeting; it was all about business, nothing personal. *I guess he's still married.* She hadn't noticed if he wore a ring; most of the time his hands were in his pocket; he taught class like that too. He'd walk around with his hands in his pockets; that was his stance. She looked at the time. It was going on six, and she was meeting Desire and Kendrick at 7:00pm.

Simone walked out on the floor and said, "Ladies, do I need a babysitter here tonight to make sure we do things right?"

They all said, "No, Ms. Simone."

Simone replied, "Okay. I will be back later tonight; I want the magazine on my desk so it can be ready to hit the newsstands next week. Overtime is available. If you decide to stay, text me so I can log it; see you later this evening." Simone called Desire to say she was on her way.

She got to the restaurant a little after seven. She saw Desire and Kendrick waiting at the bar, and she hugged them both.

"So how was your trip to the Bahamas?" Simone asked.

Desire replied, "It was awesome. You need to go."

Simone said, "If I'm going to the Bahamas it's with my man."

Desire said, "OMG! You got a man, Simone; when did this happen?"

Simone said, "Desire, really? If I had a man, I would've flown out to the Bahamas to tell you." They laughed.

Desire looked at Simone and said, "What's wrong?"

"Oh, it's nothing."

"Your nothing looks like it's something." As Simone was about to reply, Kendrick got up to answer his phone. Simone said,

"I just saw an old friend today, and it brought back some memories."

Desire said, "You want to talk about it?"

Simone said, "No, my heart has healed; I don't want to open that up again." Kendrick returned and sat down.

Kendrick said, "I have an old friend in town; he's leaving this weekend. I told him to meet us here. If that's okay?"

Desire and Simone said that was fine.

Desire said, "He can sit next to Simone, maybe they can get acquainted."

Simone rolled her eyes. "Whatever, I am not in the mood."

Just when her eyes got adjusted back into her sockets, she looked at the door and in walked Jesse. Kendrick got up, walked over to Jesse to give him a hug. Kendrick brought Jesse to the table. Jesse sat next to Simone, and her heart started fluttering again.

Simone said, "Can you excuse me?" She tapped Desire on the shoulder. It was a signal Desire knew well.

Desire said, "Excuse me. I'll be right back." They both went into the ladies' room. Simone started crying. Desire said, "What's wrong?"

Simone said, "That's him!"

"That's who?" Desire asked.

"That's the old friend I saw today," Simone replied. "I wanted to cry at work, but the ladies came in after he left. I didn't want them in my business, and when I got here to meet up with you guys, I was going to vent. Then Jesse walked in. I know I couldn't do it in front of him, that's why I came in here."

While Simone was in the bathroom with Desire, Jesse was in the men's room with Kendrick.

"OMG! That's her," Jesse said.

"That's who?"

"That's the lady I was telling you I was in love with," Jesse said.

"Simone?"

Jesse replied, "Yes, Simone!"

Kendrick said, "She's my sister-in-law. Wait a minute; does Simone know you're in love with her?"

Jesse said, "No. The last time I saw Simone, I told her I was getting married. She was hurt. I knew she was in love with me. Six months later, I knew I loved Simone. I decided not to get married after all."

Kendrick said, "So why didn't you go back to Simone?

Jesse said, "Simone told me not to ever come back. She didn't want to see me anymore. She was hurting and needed to heal from that pain. I respected that, so here I am two years later. I saw her earlier today."

"How did you manage to pull that off, when she told you not to see her anymore?"

"I paid off her business loan; I wanted to bring her some good news. Man, Kendrick, it was so good seeing her."

Kendrick said, "Are you going to tell her how you feel?"

"I don't know!"

Kendrick replied, "You need to tell her something."

Jesse said, "Does she have a man?"

Kendrick grinned. "I don't know if I should tell you."

"Please! I can't say anything if she's got somebody; I'd feel like a fool. But she's here with you two, alone—"

"Maybe her man is on a business trip."

Jesse groaned.

Kendrick took pity on him. "No, she doesn't. Plenty she could have, fine woman like her, but it seems like she's not interested. Maybe that's your fault."

"Thank God. I mean, you're right, I need to tell her." Kendrick and Jesse went back to their seats.

Desire asked Simone, "So what are you going to do?"

Simone replied, "There's nothing to do; he's married. I'm not going to ask him anything. I just came in here to vent because I'm still in love with him."

Desire replied, "I hope something good comes out of it, even if it's just closure."

"Closure for what?"

"Closure for your feelings. You need to close that part of you that loves him, so you can move on and love again."

Simone replied, "Maybe I'm meant to only love him."

Desire replied, "That's up to you, but don't entrap your heart with someone you can't have."

Simone hugged Desire and said, "Thank you for listening."

"That's what big sisters are for. Now wash your face. You don't want him to see you like this."

Simone freshened up, and they walked back to the table and sat down.

Kendrick said to Desire, "This is my friend Jesse. Jesse, this is my wife, Desire."

"Nice to meet you, Desire; I've heard so many nice things about you."

"It is nice to meet you, Jesse."

Kendrick said, "Jesse, this is my sister-in law, Simone. Simone, this is my friend Jesse."

Simone and Jesse replied at the same time, "We know each other."

Kendrick said, "Oh, really? I didn't know that." Desire and Kendrick looked at each other and winked.

Kendrick said to Jesse, "How long are you in town?"

"Another week, I'll be leaving next Saturday."

Kendrick said, "So how's married life?" Desire kicked Simone under the table; Simone looked at Desire, and Desire looked at her.

Jesse said, "No. I never got married. It wouldn't have worked out."

"Why not?"

"Because I'm in love with Simone."

Simone looked at Jesse and said. "Are you serious?"

Jesse replied, "Yes, you had my body and emotions on lockdown; I couldn't be intimate with anyone. My heart couldn't love anyone else but you. I didn't want to touch anyone. I felt like my body was arrested and you were the only one with a key to unlock me. I couldn't do anything, Simone."

Simone said, "The same thing that happened to you, happened to me. The last time we were intimate was my last time. You were the only one to touch my body, make love to me, the only one to kiss my lips. It's been two years since I've been with you. I call you my Beautiful Lover, Jesse, because that is what I want you to be more than anything. My lover, my best friend. There is no other for me. As I share my feelings with you, I am real about the love that I have only for you. You made love to me that crossed boundaries, you Richter-scaled my soul; you shook me into a different realm of intimacy, a level I've never been before. I wanted to go higher, and I knew only you could take me there."

Jesse replied, "You took me places in my soul that I knew no one could but you, Simone. I came back because I needed you to take me there again. There's no substitute for you. I can't duplicate what I felt with you with someone else. You have a way of making love with great finesse; you're territorial, and you etched your name in my heart. As long as I live, Simone, I will always want you with me, in my mind, body, and soul. I thought of you every night. As I closed my eyes, I would dream of me calling out for you; and when I opened them, you were not here. I started to cry, not just for me but also for you because you were sent to me from above, your lips sweet as honey. I throw myself at your feet and say here I am to give you the love you need. Looking into your

128

eyes, Simone, I am lost in their beauty. I find myself now in your heart, where I'll be forever. You erected a love in me so strong and powerful."

Simone replied, "I always wanted to hear you say that." Jesse wiped the tears from Simone's eyes; Kendrick wiped the tears from Desire's and kissed her forehead.

Jesse leaned over and kissed Simone and said, "I'll love you always, Simone."

Simone replied, "I'll love you forever, my Beautiful Lover."

UNREHEARSED MOAN

"Mic check 1, 2, 1,2. Hello out there, my name is Naomi; I'm your spinner for tonight; hope you like my vibe. I got some melodies I mixed together; it's a good flavor, hope you savor it. If you like my groove, and it's something you like to move to at your own party, I got contact cards waiting for you. Let me drop this beat and enjoy the evening."

Naomi was a DJ. She did parties, clubs, and weddings. She had moved down here from New Jersey a couple of months ago; she was enjoying life in Miami, Fl. She grew up in Brooklyn, NY, so music was always in her ears. She'd been to house parties, block parties; everywhere she went she was surrounded by music. She'd go to bed listening to it, wake up to it. She knew every word to a song. If she had a slot on her body, you could put a quarter in her, and she would sing you the song from beginning to end. Her voice was harmonious and smooth like butter, so her rhythm was on point. High and low note, not a problem, she was hitting it. After she graduated from college, she wanted to move away and see other styles of living. Her roommate from college, Jody, moved to Miami a year ago, so when Naomi finished college, Jody wanted her to move to Miami. For now, they were roommates. Jody had a co-worker who was having a party and needed a DJ. Since Jody knew Naomi had skills, she recommended her. Jody gave Naomi the phone number. She called to find out what type of party it was, the kind of music they liked, and how long they needed her. She set her price. Naomi had only been in town six months, but her name got around quickly; you'd think she'd been there for years. Every Saturday, she had a gig. The party Naomi was at that night lasted four hours. It was a hit. As everyone was leaving, so were her cards on the table. Naomi's price was fifty dollars an hour, so she made two hundred that night, plus tips. As she was packing up her equipment, a gentleman approached her. He said, "Hello, my name is Damian; I love the way you do your music."

Naomi said, "Thank you."

"I'm having a party in a month. I'd like to talk to you more about it," the gentleman said.

Naomi said, "That's great, but I don't have any more cards to hand out."

He pulled out his business card, handed it to her, and said, "You can write it on mine." She wrote the number and handed it back to him. He said, "You ever notice when you talk, you sing?"

She said, "I never noticed that."

He said, "I did." Amongst other things, Damian said, "Have a good night."

Naomi said, "And to you as well." Jody helped Naomi carry her equipment to the car.

"So, what was that about?" Jody said to Naomi.

Naomi said, "What was what?"

Jody said, "That little encounter there."

Naomi said, "That was about an upcoming event he wants me to play at."

Jody said, "There was a lot more to it than that!"

Naomi brushed it off. She said, "Girl, get in the car. You're always thinking up something."

Jody said, "Whatever. Why did he wait until everyone was gone to approach you?"

Naomi said, "Maybe he wanted to catch me at a time I wasn't busy. Let it ride, Jody." Jody looked at Naomi like she just got scolded by her mother, lip pouting and folding her arms. "Don't be looking at me with that attitude," Naomi said.

Jody turned her head and whispered, "I still think it's something more."

"Zip it," Naomi said.

Two days later Naomi got a call; it was Damian. "Hey there, Damian, how are you?"

He said, "I'm fine, and yourself?"

"I'm good."

Damian said, "Can we talk about the upcoming event?"

"Sure. Let's hear your proposal."

Damian said, "This event is on a yacht. It's a five-hour event. It's starts at 8:00 pm and ends at 1:00 am. It's a black-tie event. I know your fee— fifty an hour. We'll be paying you two hundred an hour."

"Wait a minute. If you're paying that much, why don't you hire a professional?"

Damian said, "I am; that's why I'm calling you. I like your style. I've heard others play before, but you bring something different, like you make love in your music."

She said, "Oh, I put music together like I do when I cook; I take my time with it, no rush. I want to make sure everything is there, so you can feel what I'm feeling when I'm doing it. I'm a master chef at what I do; I'll have you coming back for more."

Damian said, "Very impressive."

She said, "I know."

"Cocky, aren't we?"

"Only about my skills."

Damian said, "I like that." She moaned. He said, "Why do you do that?"

"What?"

He said, "Moan like that."

"Oh, I've been doing that all my life. I don't even know I'm doing it. It's like an unrehearsed moan. I do it sometimes when I'm thinking."

"What are you thinking about?"

Naomi replied, "Who knows I just do it; it's a habit."

"It's a—never mind."

Naomi said, "Finish your sentence, Damian."

Damian said nothing. He then said, "Let's get back to the event. You have a lot of equipment. We could load it up the night before; that way you don't have to bring it all on that night."

"Will it be safe there?"

"Of course. The night of the event, I'll send a limo to pick you up."

Naomi asked, "Can I bring my roommate Jody with me?"

"Sure, it's a plus one event. I don't mind if you bring a guy."

Naomi laughed and said, "Jody is a girl."

"In that case, sure, bring her along."

Naomi asked, "What kind of music would you like played."

"The way I saw you flow on those tables, you flowmetrically are on point. It's like your whole body is filled with musical notes, and you play it through your music."

"I never heard it said like that before." She moaned again.

Damian said, "You did it again."

"Did what?"

"That moan."

Naomi said, "Can I ask you something?"

"Sure."

"Does it do something to you?"

"Why do you ask?"

"Because you keep asking me why I keep doing it."

He replied, "It's just different. I've never heard anyone moan while they were talking."

Naomi said, "Talking is not the only time I moan." Damian swallowed. "We'll talk more about this event later. Jody and I are getting ready to go the movies; we'll talk soon. Have a good night."

Damian replied, "And to you as well."

Naomi hung up the phone. Jody said, "And!"

Naomi said, "And what?"

"What was that conversation about?"

"Damian was giving details about the event."

"And!"

Naomi said, "What is with you and your ands?"

"There's more to it than this."

"Girl, bye," Naomi replied. "Damian said this party is on a yacht. You want to go?"

"Girl, yes!"

"It's a black-tie event."

Jody said, "I have a black tie, I just need some slacks to go with it."

Naomi bust out laughing and said, "Girl, you are a straight fool. Black tie event means elegant."

Jody said, "Oh, okay. When are we going shopping for this black-tie event thingy?"

Naomi said, "We'll go tomorrow, to Saks or Neiman Marcus."

Jody said, "Girl, my money says Ross or Marshalls."

"I can't with you, Jody."

"Who else are you going to do it with then?" They both laughed. They headed out to the movies. Naomi didn't feel like driving downtown, so they hopped on the bus. Not even a minute after getting on, Naomi heard her name – *that's the spinner Naomi* – she turned around. There were people from the party where she met Damian.

Naomi said, "Hey guys, what's going on?"

One from the crowd said, "We're going to this club downtown, it's a new spot. I'm Joey. This is my twin sister Jennifer and my best friend Dana. We were just talking about your music?"

Naomi said, "What about it?"

"You have a smooth way of mixing beats," Joey said. Naomi blushed. "What are you guys up to?"

Naomi said, "We're on our way to the movies."

"You should come with us, see how they spin," Dana said. Naomi was never for competition; she was just good at what she did.

Naomi asked Jody, "You want to go check this out?"

Jody responded, "I'm game."

They got to their stop and there was a crowd of people waiting to get in. Naomi was not in the mood for standing in line. Dana said, "I got this, follow me." They walked up to the man at the door.

Dana said, "What's up, Steve?"

Steve responded, "What's up, Dana? How many you have tonight?"

"I've got five on it."

Steve looked at the list, let them in and said, "Enjoy the evening."

They went up to the second floor. Dana said, "I'll be right back." Naomi looked around; it was a nice club. The dance floor

136

was crowded. She saw all these pillows on the floor and had no clue what they were for. Joey said to Naomi, "You want to hit the floor?"

Naomi said, "Sure." Joey grabbed Naomi's hand, and they headed to the dance floor. Joey was showing his moves. Naomi wasn't so bad herself. The floor started to get crowded. Joey grabbed two pillows and handed Naomi one. "Countdown, 5,4,3,2,1," over the mic they heard, "FIGHT, FIGHT. FIGHT, FIGHT." A pillow fight broke out; everyone was hitting each other with pillows. With all the feathers going up in the air, it looked like snow falling. Naomi couldn't see anything, there were so many feathers and it was a little dark. The next thing she heard was, "Hello, Moaner." She turned around to see who said it. So many feathers were around, she couldn't see who it was, so she kept hitting Joey and others with the pillows. The fight lasted for thirty minutes. After it was over, Jody and Naomi headed home. Naomi laughed all the way home, she had so much fun.

Saturday morning came quickly since they got home at 3:00 am. Naomi asked Jody, "What time do you want to go shopping?" The event was three weeks away, and Naomi wanted to get the shopping out of the way.

Jodie said, "If we are going to Neiman's, I'll window shop."

Naomi said, "Girl, just come on." They headed out at 12:00 pm. They got to the mall and had lunch first. Naomi never liked to shop on an empty stomach. They finished lunch and headed for Neiman's. Before they went in, Jody said, "I smell the prices from

137

here, and they smell—sniff, sniff, sniff—like new car smell: Expensive!" Naomi grabbed Jody, pulled her into the store and said, "Stop playing; we're just looking." Naomi asked the saleslady for dresses for the event. She pointed to the fine dresses area, and they walked over. Naomi looked at the tags and smiled. Jody looked at the tags and almost fainted. Naomi saw a cute, short dress with a cut-out in the back. She'd be spinning that night, but the dress was so worth wearing.

Three hundred dollars: it was marked down. Jody said they need to mark it down some more. Naomi tried it on; she had the cutest figure. Jody said, "Can you put it on layaway?"

Naomi said, "You don't put anything on layaway; not in this store. I'm getting it."

Jody said, "You paid your rent already; you can get it." Naomi gave her a smirk and went to the register to pay for it. The cashier rang it up, put it in a bag, and handed Naomi the receipt.

"Wait a minute. I didn't pay for it!"

The cashier said, "No, you didn't, but it is paid for, you have the receipt in your hand." Jody quickly grabbed a dress; she wanted to see if it would work for her too. The cashier rung it up, handed Jody the receipt. Naomi said, "If I knew it was going to be like this, I would've picked shoes too."

The cashier said, "The limit on this card is one thousand dollars; you have four hundred remaining."

Naomi said, "What card?"

The cashier responded, "I can't say but someone thinks you're special." They looked around for some shoes and accessories and spent every dime of what was left on the card. They went home and talked about the mystery of their shopping spree.

Naomi's phone rang, and she answered. "Hello."

"Hey there, Naomi. It's Damian," he said.

"What's going on?"

Damian replied, "There's been a change of plans; the party has been moved back. It will be next weekend. That's not too short of a notice, is it?"

"Wow, no, perfect timing. I just bought my dress today."

Damian said, "That's great. We can meet that Friday and load your equipment on the boat."

"Okay." Naomi and Jody scheduled appointments to get their hair and nails done on that Saturday morning. That following Friday, they rode out to the marina to meet Damian.

He waved from the yacht, "Come aboard, ladies." He sent some men down to get her equipment. Naomi and Jody went aboard, and Damian greeted them.

Naomi said, "This yacht is huge."

"It's one of the largest in the area. You girls want a tour?"

They replied, "Sure." It was a thirty-minute tour, then they came back to where Naomi would be playing. It looked like a studio where you lay down tracks. It was facing the dance floor. She loved it—just her and her music in this room. Naomi said to Damian, "Thank you so much for inviting me to play."

Damian replied, "Don't thank me just yet." Naomi moaned, and so did Damian. He walked Naomi and Jody down to her car and waved to them as they drove off. Saturday morning, when the ladies were in the salon, Damian called Naomi. "What are you doing, getting pretty for tonight?"

Naomi replied, "Yes, I like to be on time. I don't like to rush or be rushed."

Damian said, "That's my girl. What salon are you at?" She gave him the address, and twenty minutes later he dropped in. Jody looked at Naomi to see her reaction. There was none; Jody rolled her eyes up in her head. Damian said, "It's my treat for you ladies." Naomi and Jody looked at each other, and at the same time they said, Okay! Three hours later they finished up and headed back home to get some rest.

Naomi was excited about the party. She could barely sleep. She'd done big parties before, but this was her first time on a yacht. Going through her music collection in her mind, she finally drifted off to sleep. Jody shook her three hours later. "Naomi, wake up, girl, it's six o clock." Naomi got up, jumped in the shower. She was good with makeup; what took some women twenty minutes to do, she did in five. She slipped on that sexy black dress, panty hosed up the legs, stilettoed the feet.

Naomi said, "All we need is the red carpet to walk down."

"Beep, beep." The limo was outside, Naomi and Jody walked towards the limo like movie stars, got in, and off to the party they went. While in the car, Naomi was going over her list of music to play; she was excited and nervous at the same time. She closed her eyes to nap for the forty-five-minute drive. They arrived at the party, stepped out of the car and there it was, a red carpet, waiting for them all the way up to the steps of the yacht. Naomi thought, *what kind of party is this; photographers taking pictures like they are the paparazzi.* They walked on board.

People everywhere, glasses of wine, champagne; you name it, they were drinking it. Damian walked up to Naomi, kissed her on the cheek. "You ready?"

She replied, "I always am." Damian introduced Naomi to the crowd, grabbed her hand and escorted her up the stairs. Naomi whispered into the mic, "Good evening!" She moaned. All the men gave her their undivided attention; the ladies were still mingling, but the men had their eyes glued to her. Her moan was like a dog whistle; only the men could hear it. Damian noticed it as well. He looked at Naomi. She was just herself; she was beautiful in his eyes, but objectively her looks weren't out of the ordinary.

Naomi didn't know her unrehearsed moan was erotic. She put on her earphones, and off she spun. The yacht began moving as soon as she spun the first song. Damian brought her a glass of champagne. He said, "When this party is over, I want to show you something."

She said, "That will be fine."

Damian replied, "Yes, you are."

Naomi smiled. She put a list of songs on automatic play, so she could mingle with the crowd, grab something to eat. She went over to the buffet table. Many approached her, mostly men; she was the life of the party. Damian sat back and watched; he wanted to see how she would handle them. She conversed with a few, fixed her plate and walked away. Naomi was not a needy woman; she didn't like a lot of attention; she didn't need it. She was very independent but would like companionship. She knew how to draw a crowd but disappeared in it. Damian liked what he saw; her body language spoke volumes, as if she was already spoken for. The party was a hit as always; Naomi made her mark again.

The boat docked at exactly 1:00 am. Naomi packed up her equipment. Damian said, "We can move that tomorrow; I have something to show you."

Damian, Naomi, and Jody got in the limo. Damian said to Naomi, "I hope we have a trust relationship?"

She responded, "I believe we do."

Damian replied, "Can I blindfold you?"

Naomi said, "Yes, you can, because Jody is here; I know she won't let anything happen to me." He blindfolded her. They took a thirty-minute ride to their destination. Damian helped Naomi out of the car; he guided her. When it was time to step up, he told her; when it was time to step down, he let her know. It was real quiet. Damian said, "We are walking up some stairs, there are ten of them." She counted as she went up them. They walked down the hall, and she heard Damian open a door. He said, "We are almost there, just a couple of steps more, and stop."

Damian slowly took the blindfold off and whispered in her ear, "Hello, Moaner." She turned around with this surprised look on her face.

Damian kissed her. After a one-minute kiss, she asked, "What's going on, Damian!"

He said, "When I heard you moan at the party, I was attracted to you. You aroused me in many ways I had never felt before; I had to have you. You met my sister Dana; she's my twin. She told me you were here that night. I was in the other booth next to this one. This is my club. I own it. When I saw you having fun with the pillow fight, I snuck down to say hello to you. Dana also told me where you'd be shopping the next day. I got there early to leave my credit card with the cashier—she's a friend of Dana's—so you could buy something pretty. You have on the dress I hoped you'd pick."

Damian went on to say, "I brought you here because I want you to spin for me. I love your style; you draw a crowd; your essence is so sensual. I want to bottle it up and disperse it into the atmosphere, like a fragrance. You have a way of bringing people together through your voice and music—that unrehearsed moan of yours is hypnotic. The party on the boat was celebrating my success, and I wanted you to be a part of everything. With that being said; do you like my offer?

"Oh, I didn't tell you how much I'd be paying you? It's thirty-five hundred every two weeks, but since you will be my lady soon, you'll receive much more than that. So, do you like my offer?"

143

"Like it? I love it."

Damian said, "So I can write up your contract?

"I would like that."

Damian replied, "We can't mix business with pleasure, and since you're not on the clock right now, I'd like to kiss you again."

Naomi replied, "I'd like that too." Damian kissed her, and she passionately moaned.

Damian said, "Oh, I like that."

"If you notice, my name Naomi; spelled backwards it reads 'I moan.' I guess I got the right name."

Damian said, "You got the right everything."

PAPER PROOF

With eight months left on the lease, Michael informed Samaya that he would not be renewing it. She'd have to either find a roommate or find something she can afford. They had shared an apartment for three years. Their relationship had ended, and he was buying a condo. Michael had given her enough time to save up some money. Samaya had it good, maybe too good.

Michael and Samaya were introduced by mutual friends. It wasn't for a date. Michael had just moved into his apartment, and Samaya had just been evicted from hers; she had a six-month-old baby girl named Chelsea. Samaya had been staying at a shelter until she could find a place to stay.

Michael's co-workers were friends of Samaya's; they were talking about the situation to him, not so that he would pity her; it was just in a general conversation. Michael thought more about the baby than the mother. He had a two-year-old son named Tyler; he and his ex-wife shared custody. Michael got Tyler every other weekend; the bedroom was already set up for occupancy.

Michael began to ask questions about Samaya: what type of person was she? Did she have a job, did she have a criminal background? Hopefully, she's not a serial killer. They laughed. No, she's not one of those. She was going to school for nursing, trying to work and go to school at the same time, but she couldn't find a

145

babysitter to watch her daughter. Michael thought what harm could she do with a six-month-old baby? Michael said, "I have a spare bedroom. They could stay with me until she gets on her feet. She can sleep in Tyler's room. Tyler can sleep with me when he comes for the weekend."

The co-worker asked, "You sure it's not going to be an inconvenience?"

"No, plus she has a little girl. I always wanted a daughter. Well, this won't be my daughter, but I always wanted a little girl. The baby is still an infant, at least I'll have a little girl while she's staying with me, so no, I don't mind at all." Samaya received the news, and after making sure Michael was a good guy, trustworthy, she moved in the following Saturday. Michael went over some ground rules. He let her know she was only there temporarily until she could make it on her own. She agreed, and Michael asked Samaya about the babysitting arrangements.

She replied that she was almost finished with school; she had a promising position after she completed her course.

Michael asked, "What hours will you be working?"

"Eight to five." Michael worked at night.

"To help you out so you don't have to pay daycare fees, if you trust me, I'll watch Chelsea while you work. I'll pay all the bills here; you can save your money." She thought that was special, and she did trust Michael. She could tell right away he was a good man. She finished school in a month, and the plan Michael put together went into effect immediately. Michael was all about order.

He was an army brat; his father had raised him like he was in boot camp. He also taught him how to be a man. Michael was precise about everything, even how he kept his place. You'd think he was a woman or an interior decorator—his place looked like someone from that field put it together.

Samaya loved how his place looked. She had never seen anything like it before. She respected everything about Michael. He could put an apartment together, but not a meal; he had more frozen dinners in his freezer than ice cubes. On the other hand, that was Samaya's specialty. He gave her a warm and cozy place to stay, and she gave him a warm meal; it was a perfect combination. It was really working out for them both. Michael was growing quite fond of Chelsea. He was teaching her how to walk, teaching her ABCs. When his son Tyler would come over, he'd act like the big brother.

Michael and Samaya were both home on the weekends. They weren't dating anyone, so they'd interact with each other like they were a family. When Chelsea turned a year old, they went out to celebrate her birthday. Michael and Samaya looked like a cute couple, although neither one of them thought about dating each other. The original plan was the same. Samaya was still saving her money to move, Michael was still helping her out. That would change two months later.

Samaya was in the kitchen cooking, when Michael walked in. He asked Samaya, "What's for dinner?"

She replied, "Lasagna."

"It smells good."

"Thank you."

Michael then asked, "Why aren't you dating anyone?"

"I was going to ask the same thing about you."

Michael said, "Well since you were staying here, I didn't want to disrespect you and bring someone here. I just wouldn't feel right."

"I appreciate that, but this is your place. I'm just here temporarily."

Michael replied, "I understand that, but that's just me."

Samaya said, "I would never bring anyone here; it's not my place to do that. Plus, my daughter has gotten so used to seeing you, I don't want to confuse her. Although you're just watching her, she doesn't need to see another man around me."

Michael replied, "That makes perfect sense. Let's date each other then."

Samaya looked at him and smiled. She said, "I thought about that, but I didn't want to say anything."

Michael said, "It will work out fine. My son knows you; Chelsea knows me. We are not strangers to each other; I think it will work." Samaya agreed.

She asked, "So do we split the bills? What happens now?"

Michael replied, "Nothing changes. You can still save your money, and if things go well with us, we may buy a house one day." She smiled; she liked how he took control of things. Michael then said, "We have a boy and a girl. I'm not looking to have any more children; I like what we have, and I'd like to keep it that way." He asked her if she was on the control. Samaya nodded. He said, "Okay then we can move on and see how this turns out."

He walked up to Samaya, gave her a hug and a kiss, and she said, "Oh, you can kiss."

"You took the words right out of my mouth."

Samaya said, "Let me see what else I can get out of it." She kissed him again. "Hmmm, I love it."

He replied, "Me too."

Samaya said, "We have to be discreet around our kids until they are old enough to understand what's going on." Michael agreed. While Chelsea was sleep, Samaya slept in Michael's room. She had never been in there before. They were roommates, and there was no need to go in; now that they were in a relationship, she'd be going in there more often.

Their relationship skyrocketed. Michael was starting to have feelings for Samaya. He started introducing her to family and friends. He was happy and content. He let his guard down fast with her; he just knew it would be something permanent. They had been dating about a year now. Chelsea was growing up, and Samaya put her in daycare. Michael changed his hours, so he could be home with Samaya and Chelsea in the evening. They shared days picking Chelsea up from daycare. If she had to work late, it was Michael's day to pick her up.

Michael got home and put some food on for Chelsea. He needed something from the store, so he called Samaya on her cellphone. It went straight to voicemail. He called her job and they said she had left at 5:00 pm. Michael had thought that strange; she was supposed to be working until 9:00 pm. He called her on her cell again, straight to voicemail. He was a little upset, but he didn't show it in front of Chelsea. He fed her dinner, gave her a bath, and read her a book for her sleepy time. Her bedtime was promptly at 8:00 pm.

Chelsea was down for the count. He kissed her on the cheek, turned the light off, and cracked the door in case she needed to use the bathroom or get a drink of water. He lay across his bed to watch TV. He called her cell again; it went straight to voicemail. He looked at his watch; it was 9:15 pm. Then he heard someone at the door. It was Samaya. She walked into his bedroom and said, "Hey, baby." She walked up to Michael and gave him a kiss.

"I tried calling you on your cell, to let you know Chelsea needed some juice and to pick some up on the way home." He didn't tell her he called her job; he wanted to see how this played out.

She replied, "Oh, we had to turn our phones off. We were on a different floor where radiation is, and I wasn't at my regular station. Did Chelsea eat?"

"Yes, and she had her bath."

She asked, "How was your day?"

"It was good."

She asked, "You want a massage? I got some oils for you."

He said, "Oh, heck yeah." They took a shower together, and she gave him a good massage, put him right to sleep. She was hoping it wouldn't end otherwise tonight, and she got her wish. The next morning, Samaya was in the kitchen making Chelsea something to eat. Michael was still sleep. He was awakened by her cell phone; he didn't pay it any attention until it rang again. It must be important, he thought. He didn't answer it, he just looked at who was calling. *My little secret* was the name. He said, *hmmm*, put the phone down, and tried to go back to sleep. He heard a message being left; it was a text. He looked at her phone again. *I hope it's my baby, I love you.*

Michael was wide awake now. Who's having whose baby? Just when he thought that, in walked Chelsea to give Michael a hug. "Good morning, Miguel." She couldn't say Michael, so she called him Miguel.

He responded, "Good morning, Chelsea boo, how are you?"

"Fine." Michael really loved Chelsea. He known her since she was six months old and now she was two. Her father wasn't in her life, so he kind of took that place, and he felt like it too. He would do anything for Chelsea.

Samaya came in the room and said, "Good morning, baby."

"Good morning."

Samaya said to Chelsea, "Grab your rain boots; it's raining out."

"Okay, Mommy."

Michael said, "Are you working late again tonight?"

"Yes, but I'll pick Chelsea up. I'm doing a split shift."

"I can pick her up; it's no problem."

Samaya responded, "Are you sure?"

"Yes, I'm sure."

Samaya said, "Okay." She kissed Michael, went to get Chelsea so she could drop her off to day care, came back in the room to grab her phone, and said, "Later, babes."

"Later." He was trying to make sense of the text that was on her phone. Maybe it was the wrong number. Michael was good to Samaya; there would be no reason she would cheat on him, and he brushed that thought off. He took the day off from work. He wanted to surprise her for her birthday. It was tomorrow, but he wanted to surprise her early, so later that afternoon, he went to her job to take her out to lunch.

He asked for her, and which floor she was working on. One of the nurses replied Samaya was on vacation and wouldn't be back until Monday. Michael was furious. He thought how could she be on vacation if she'd been home every night? He called her cell, straight to voicemail. He didn't understand what was going on. What did he do wrong? He was just too good to her, but why would she mess something up like this? Where could she be during the day?

He went by Chelsea's daycare to pick her up. Chelsea said, "Hey, it's Miguel." She always put a smile on Michael's face.

He said to Chelsea, "You want to go for some ice cream?"

Chelsea said, "Yes, yes, Miguel."

He said, "Let's go get some then." She really made his heart melt. She was so cute and innocent. They went downtown. After they ate ice cream, Michael took her to the store to get her a pair of new shoes. Michael bought all of Chelsea's clothes. He dressed her; yeah, he was the daddy; he always wanted a little girl. Chelsea just happened to fill that spot.

Chelsea said to Michael, "I have to go to potty."

He said, "Okay." He didn't want to send her in the ladies' bathroom by herself, so he took her in the men's bathroom. As they were going in, there was a man coming out. Chelsea said, "Hello, Mr. Mark."

He looked down and said, "Hello, Chelsea. How are you?"

"I got ice cream," she replied, giggling. The man walked on.

Michael and Chelsea went in the restroom. Michael asked Chelsea, "How do you know that man?"

Chelsea replied, "That's mommy's boyfriend!" Michael couldn't believe what he heard. As they were leaving the store, Michael saw Samaya and Mark having a conversation. She looked stressed, and she quickly left, leaving Mark standing there.

Michael walked up to Mark and asked, "Wasn't that Chelsea's mom you were talking to?"

Mark replied, "Yes."

"She seemed awfully quick to run off."

Mark replied, "Yeah, I told her I saw Chelsea. She told me to describe you, I did, and she ran off. Are you Chelsea's dad?"

"Yes. I'm also Samaya's man!"

Mark looked crazy in the face. "She told me she was single!"

Michael asked, "How long have you been seeing her?"

"About three months. She told me that she's pregnant."

"Oh, really!"

"Yes." Michael thanked Mark for the information. Michael and Chelsea left the mall.

Michael asked Chelsea, "Did you enjoy your ice cream?"

"Yes. More!"

"Not today, sweetie. Shall we go home?"

"Okay, Daddy."

"We need to stop by the store and pick you up some juices for your dinner."

She said, "Yay, I love juices." Michael stopped by the store to pick up some items, and they headed home. When they got there, Samaya was in the kitchen cooking dinner. She came out of the kitchen and greeted Chelsea and Michael. She kissed Michael and gave Chelsea a hug.

Chelsea said, "Mommy, I seen Mark!" She looked like she had just gotten the worse news ever.

Michael asked, "Who's Mark, Samaya?"

"He's a co-worker." She then asked Chelsea, "Are you ready to eat?"

Chelsea replied, "I had ice cream. I'm not hungry."

Samaya asked, "Do you want to take your bath now?"

"Yes. I want Miguel to give me my bath." Samaya looked puzzled. Michael walked by her like a proud daddy. He picked

Chelsea up, took her in the room so she could pick out her pajamas, ran her bath water, put her favorites bubbles in the bath. They sang "Row, Row, Row, Your Boat." Samaya went back in the kitchen to finish dinner. Michael finished up the bath with Chelsea and read her a bedtime story. She was sleep by 7:30. Michael usually cracked the door, but tonight he closed it. He kept his eye on the door and his ears open. If Chelsea had to come out, he would hear her.

Michael walked in the kitchen and asked how her day was?

She replied. "It was good. I got off early today, wasn't feeling good."

"I hope you feel better." She finished dinner. Michael ate, she cleaned up the kitchen, and they relaxed on the couch.

Michael said, "I went by your job today. I wanted to take you out for your birthday. I know it's tomorrow. Funny thing; your co-worker told me you were on vacation. I know you didn't talk to me about that, so I knew you were up to something. I took Chelsea to get some ice cream and ran into someone named Mark. He wouldn't happen to be your *little secret*, would he? That name came up on your phone when that person called this morning."

Michael was just rambling on, not giving Samaya any room to talk. He was very calm. "I had an interesting conversation with Mark after I took Chelsea to the restroom; I just want to confirm some things with you." Samaya was squirming.

Michael asked, "What's wrong?"

She replied, "I have to use the restroom."

Michael said, "*PERFECT TIMING*!" He went inside the grocery bag and took out a pregnancy test. He said, "Go pee on this for me."

Samaya looked crazy. She said, "What do you mean by that?"

Michael replied, "Well, if it comes up negative, we have a lot to talk about. If it's positive, we definitely have a lot to talk about." She snatched the test. Michael said, "I'll stand here and watch, to make sure you do it right." She rolled her eyes. She peed on the stick, wrapped it in tissue, and handed it to Michael. He waited two minutes and looked at it; it was positive. She came out of the bathroom. Michael said, "Sit down, I want to share something with you." He handed her the stick and went in his bedroom.

Michael unlocked his safe, moved his gun to the side, retrieved an envelope, and went back in the living room. He said to Samaya, "I told you at the beginning of our relationship that I didn't want any more children, said I was fine with what we had; remember when I said that to you?" She nodded. "Did you look at the results of that test?" Michael asked.

She said, "Yes."

"What did it say?"

"Positive."

Michael said, "Yes, it's positive, and I'm positive it's not mine."

Samaya said, "How do you know that?"

Michael replied, "Because I have paper proof."

Samaya asked, "What does that mean?" Michael pulled out this paper in the envelope and showed the date of his vasectomy that was done three years ago. "I had this done because I knew I didn't want any more children after my son, so nobody could trick me and say it was mine. Since I now know you cheated on me, I can no longer trust you. I do want to be in Chelsea's life; she has done nothing wrong to me. I adore that little girl. You have eight months to find you somewhere to stay. I hope you have saved enough money to stabilize yourself. If there is anything Chelsea needs, I will be there for her. If you allow me, I would like to get her on weekends so you she can spend time with me and Tyler.

"I'm not going to let you ruin what I have with Chelsea because you choose to live your life any kind of way. I will still pay the bills. I am still going to be a man about this. If you didn't have Chelsea, you'd be on the other side of my door tonight, but I love that little girl. She's done nothing to me, but if you jeopardize that child in any way, if anyone hurts or abuses her, I will get custody of her. I have the right people to get the job done, and since her biological father is not in her life, it shouldn't be problem. Do you understand what I'm saying?" Samaya nodded.

"You know what? I'm going to be the better man; you can keep this apartment. I really don't want Chelsea to move from place to place; she is your saving grace. I'll set it up, so you can get your name on the lease and I'll take mine off. I can find somewhere to stay, and you can keep everything in this apartment; call it a gift. When I do leave, you can get all the bills put in your name. I wish you the best. After tonight, I have nothing else to say to you. We can go back to being roommates until I leave. You don't have to cook me dinner; I can fend for myself. You just make sure you feed my little girl."

Eight months later, Michael found a condo and fixed up Chelsea's and Tyler's room. Samaya had her baby, a boy. Michael went over to the apartment to pick Chelsea up. Samaya answered the door with a bruise under her eye. Michael didn't ask questions. He walked past her, into Chelsea's room. Chelsea said, "Hi, Papa Bear."

Michael responded, "Hello, Chelsea boo. Are you ready to go with Papa?"

Chelsea responded, "Yes!"

Michael got custody of Chelsea when Mark, Samaya's boyfriend, turned out to be an abuser. Michael didn't want Chelsea around that. Michael kept his word; he said he would get custody of her if she was around any abuse or if anything happened to her. Chelsea now lives with Michael. He is a proud father of two.

WHATEVER IT TAKES

Caution would be his approach about love. He had a wound still healing from a pain he encountered without invitation. His plan was to love Michelle forever, but forever was not in her plan. James loved Michelle with all his heart; Michelle had other plans for hers. The day of the wedding, James waited at the altar for her. After a half an hour had passed, James knew she wasn't coming. He slowly walked down the aisle past the audience waiting for the bride to appear.

He stood outside on the church steps waiting to see if she would show up. The bride was a no show; he knew he would not see her today, or ever again. Too embarrassed to go back in, he got in the awaiting limo and rode off. He texted his best man to make the announcement the wedding was off. James went straight to the airport. Although there wouldn't be a honeymoon, he was going to Aruba anyway. He sat at the airport until it was time to take off.

James had two round trip tickets. He didn't want the other one to go to waste. He called his best friend, Tracy, to join him. He needed her to be there; she had always been there for James. The plane wasn't leaving for another five hours, so she had plenty of time to get there. James changed the name on the ticket, so it would be ready when Tracy arrived.

James didn't bother to call Michelle. He didn't want to think about her. The night before, he knew she wasn't going to show; she had cheated on him right after they got engaged. Although she said she loved him, her actions proved that her words were a lie. But no matter how she felt, James still loved her.

James was a good man; he had showed her that. He knew that's what she needed; he also thought he could find a good woman in church. Boy, was he fooled. James and Michelle met at a singles ministry some years ago. It was dating game night. You would pick a number out of a glass bowl. The ladies and men had different bowls to pick from. They would each pick a number and find the table with that number on it. The ladies would go first. They would sit at the table until the man with the same number for that table was seated.

You would introduce yourself, talk for about an hour. If you felt it was a match, you would exchange numbers and plan a date; if not, then you would come back another Saturday and try it again. The dating game was held twice a month on Saturday. Everyone looked forward to it. It became so popular, other single ministries were doing it as well. The ministry was full of single people, so they looked forward to the event.

James didn't date a lot. He was typical about what type of woman he wanted; she not only had to be beautiful, she had to have class, be smart and funny, have a sense of humor; she had to be spiritual and know how to change the atmosphere when he was feeling a certain way. She needed to be able to pick up any sadness and change it quickly. James was good at that, and he wanted someone who could also do that.

James met Michelle before they got to a table. They struck up a conversation waiting in line; the attraction was mutual, so they left the event and talked more over a cup of coffee. There was chemistry—not enough, as it turned out, but it was there. They dated about a year. Love was expressed, and the engagement ring was bought. James was tired of waiting to find the perfect woman, and he thought Michelle and he had a good thing. James thought that's what she felt, too, until the night at the movies.

Michelle let James know she had to work late. She wouldn't make it over until later that night. James called Tracy to see if she wanted to go to the movies. They met up there. The theater was dark. James and Tracy found seats closer to the screen. Minutes later he heard laughter that sounded familiar, then he heard her voice, Michelle's voice. Tracy grabbed him. She said, "Don't you move; let's hear where this conversation is going."

The man's voice said, "I love you, Michelle."

Michelle said, "I love you more."

Tracy held onto James. "Don't you move." James couldn't believe what he had just heard. He knew Michelle loved him. Was this a joke, was he being pranked? Michelle didn't know James was in the theater. The worst thing was, the wedding was tomorrow. Tracy looked at James. She said, "I know you are hurting right now, but whatever it takes to make that pain go away,

I'll be here for you." Those were comforting words to James; he could always depend on Tracy. That's why she was his best friend.

Tracy was caressing James' hand; her touch was soothing to his soul. When the movie was over, Tracy and James waited until the theater was empty.

Tracy asked James, "What are you going to do?"

James replied, "I know she loves me. We will go ahead as planned. There must be an explanation." His heart was bruised, but he couldn't believe it was over.

"Mmm-hmm," said Tracy. "You think she will show up?"

James said, "I'm not sure of anything right now. I can't call it off; the wedding is tomorrow."

Tracy said, "I hope it does turn out okay, but in my gut, James, I don't think it will."

James got a text from Michelle. She said she was still stuck at work, but she couldn't wait to marry him tomorrow. James showed Tracy the text. Tracy wasn't buying it.

She said, "We will see tomorrow."

Now, tomorrow had come, no Michelle, no wedding. He was on his way to his honeymoon without a wife. Tracy walked up to James, gave him a hug, and asked, "How are you, my friend?"

James responded, "I'm maintaining."

"I have something for you."

"What is it?" Tracy handed him an envelope. He opened it, and there was a letter along with the engagement ring. It read:

Dear James, I'm sorry I had to end it this way. I'm not in love with you. I didn't want to live a lie. I know I couldn't love you the way you needed to be loved. It's best that it happened now and not later. I do wish you the best, James, you deserved to be loved. I hope she'll love you as much as you give. Sincerely, Michelle.

James asked Tracy, "When did you get this?"

Tracy responded, "She dropped by my house when she couldn't find you at yours. I was at home packing for this trip; she knocked on my door and handed this to me. I didn't question her; it wasn't my place. What was important to me was to get here to you and make sure you were okay; right now, you need me, and that's all that matters."

James replied, "I appreciate that."

"That's what best friends are for." James took out his phone, looked up Michelle's number and hit the delete button. He deleted her out of his phone, and he wished he could delete her out of his heart. Tracy asked James, "Are you okay?"

"I will be."

"I did try on the ring. It fit perfectly."

James said, "You can have it!"

Tracy said, "I don't want no one's leftovers. If it wasn't bought for me then it's not for me." James smiled. It was time to board the plane. He handed Tracy her ticket. She said, "Oh, we're flying first class."

James said, "I only give the best. I give what I expect in return."

"You are always like that."

"And I will continue to remain that way, no plans on changing." Tracy smiled.

After they sat down on the plane, Tracy asked, "What are you going to do with that big house?"

James said, "What do you mean? I'm going to live in it."

"But it will just be you in it."

"I can manage. It's just a house." James had his house built on two acres of land. He had good taste in everything. He needed room to display his artwork since he painted for a living. Some of his pictures were in museums; he sold them for a nice piece of change and they were worth it too. He painted like he was, very emotional.

Tracy had seen James paint many times. He painted like he was making love to a woman, and he held the canvas like it was her back. The stroke of his paintbrush moved in a deep and sensual way. Tracy was caught up, watching; she was stroking her wine glass like it was the sweat off her man's back, dripping in the heat of passion. She could feel the tranquility in the atmosphere. When James painted, he set the mood just right He lit a few candles, dimmed the lights, and with aromatherapy flowing through the air, he would paint for hours. Tracy would sit there and get lost in the moment. She wouldn't tell James, but that was her seductive getaway. When James said he was painting, Tracy would come over. He'd have a chill bottle of wine waiting on her. Tracy was supportive when it came to James; she went to all his exhibits. She

164

was his right-hand woman. Tracy was a realtor; she sold James the land his house was built on. That's how they got to know each other.

They met when Tracy was at one of his exhibits, and she was asking about a piece of art he painted. He sold her the painting, and she gave him her card. He called her one-day inquiring about some property. They spent a lot of time together, looking at different properties, and they talked a lot, business and personal. Finally, she found the property he was looking for, and she made a good commission.

James took Tracy out to celebrate. They had been best friends ever since. At the time he was looking for property, James was seeing Michelle. Tracy had just finalized her divorce, but their friendship was prospering into something greater.

They arrived in Aruba and went to their hotel room. Because the reservation was already made, there was only one king-size bed to sleep in. Tracy said, "It's no problem; we're friends. I don't have a problem if you don't, James."

He replied, "I'm fine with it." They unpacked and headed out to get something to eat.

Tracy said, "It's beautiful here; I've never been anywhere like this before."

"I travel all the time; places like this are like home to me."

Tracy responded, "That must be nice."

"It is." He then asked Tracy, "What happened after I left the church?"

165

Tracy said, "After Sean got your text, he made the announcement that the wedding was canceled. We went to the reception, danced and ate; we didn't want the food to go to waste. I took all your presents to your house. Oh, by the way, here is your key."

James said, "You can keep it."

"For what?"

James replied, "Well, I didn't get married. You've been coming over, so just keep it. You know my house is your house, I have no secrets."

Tracy said, "For now, I'll hold onto it. When you find that special lady, I'll give it back to you."

"Keep it. I'm not in no rush for anyone right now." After dinner they took a walk on the beach.

Tracy asked James, "How are you feeling?"

"I'm still in shock. But I'll manage. She hurt me, but she didn't break me. I just know to be more cautious the next time. I'll pay attention to what I want. I never wrote on Michelle's heart."

Tracy said, "Explain that, please."

"We weren't connected. I loved her, but I wasn't in love with her. She had qualities that were likable, but I wasn't in love. We had a beginning, but I didn't see an end with her. I should have known better than to ask her to marry me. There was no story written with her in it. I knew she wasn't going to etch my name in her heart, so I knew not to write hers on mine. She was closed-up. She wasn't letting me in. It was shallow love; we couldn't go deeper if we tried. I don't force my love on anyone, Tracy; if you want it I will give it freely. My love has levels."

"Define that, please," Tracy asked.

James replied, "If you pull it out of me, then I know you want it, you want me. I can only give you what you extract from me. If I feel you don't want it, I stop. I don't love you less, but I won't love you more. I'll love you by how much you pull out of me. If I feel your energy, you'll feel my force, but they both must come together. I can't give you warmth, and you give me the chill factor. The energy must be the same and remain. I need to know that we both want the same thing. Tracy, do you understand what I'm saying now?"

Tracy gasped and whispered, "I do." She was mesmerized. She was lost in what James was saying. It was almost like he was painting but this time with words instead of a paintbrush; he was stroking her soul delicately.

James said, "Are you ready to go back to the room?"

"Yes, I am." James had a certain respect for Tracy. He didn't approach her like he did other women. He really liked Tracy; she was spunky; she knew what she wanted in life, and she worked until she got it. He admired her ambition. She was a go-getter. They made it back to the room and took turns showering. Tracy was in the bed when James came out the bathroom; she was checking her phone for appointments.

James lay across the bed. He grabbed Tracy's foot and began tickling it. She said, "That's a sensitive spot."

167

"How sensitive?"

She replied, "Sensitive enough to bite my lip."

James responded, "Oh, that sensitive."

"Yes, I have other spots too."

"Hmm," James said. Tracy changed the subject quick.

She said, "James, I know you have gone through some things. I will be your antidote for you to heal, your ear when you need to talk, your mouth when you need to be encouraged. I will be the arms to hold you when you need to be comforted. Whatever it takes, I will be here for you."

James said, "You changed the atmosphere when you showed up at the airport. My whole demeanor changed when you came. I needed you here with me. I couldn't do this trip by myself; I would've been calling Michelle, trying to get answers, but not once did I think about her with you here."

"You know I'm your sunshine on a cloudy day."

James responded, "You've always been that, no matter how I'm feeling, Tracy. When I call you, you change my attitude; The minute I hear your voice, I have this peace in my spirit."

"I never knew that."

"Now you do."

"And it's good to know that. Goodnight, my friend," Tracy said.

"Good night," James replied. In the morning they headed out for breakfast. They enjoyed all the festivities for newlyweds; they went scuba diving, got couple massages; Tracy had cucumbers on her eyes. James took one off and ate it. She thought that was cute. Then he grabbed one out of the bowl and put it on her eye.

Tracy asked, "Why didn't you just grab that one out the bowl and eat it?"

"I wanted to taste the cucumber from your skin to see if it had a different taste."

"Did it?"

James replied, "Indeed so." After the massages, they did a little shopping. James bought this cute bracelet for Tracy; it said friends for a lifetime, with two hearts connecting. James said, "You will always be my friend." Tracy saw a sparkle in James's eye when he said it, it was almost like a confirmation sparkle. They went to lunch after shopping, then ran on the beach like lovers, kicking up water.

James kicked water on Tracy, and she pushed him in the water. He ran and grabbed her and threw her in the water. They laughed; they both needed that carefree moment. When they took pictures, James and Tracy looked like a couple.

One man, part of a couple, said to James, "You have a beautiful wife."

James replied, "Thank you." Tracy smiled. James noticed the glow on Tracy's face. He knew it had nothing to do with the facial she just had. He had noticed it yesterday.

Tracey said, "You didn't spare any expense for this trip. Michelle missed out."

"Somethings are not meant for everyone, just someone." Tracy agreed.

"Thank you for the invitation," Tracy said.

"Oh, my pleasure. One thing I like about you, Tracy, you never ask for anything."

"I'm not supposed to; you're my best friend."

"I understand that, but you're so genuine. It's like I already know what you want. When I offer it, you take it with gratitude?"

"I'm not picky about anything. If you offer it, that's what I take. I'm not choosy about what is given to me. Whatever you choose for me to have, that's what I accept. If that's what you think of me, that's what you give me."

James said, "I would never think less of you or give you less."

Tracy said, "I know; it was just a metaphor. You give, how you would like it returned, right?

"Yes."

"I know you won't give less." Tracy walked on, and James walked behind her, admiring her beauty. She swayed as she walked, very womanly. He liked a lot of things about Tracy; he just didn't tell her. They headed back to the room to pack up. The little getaway was over for them, but they were taking something back with them.

On the plane, James thought a lot about Tracy. She had been there all the time. Tracy comforted him at the movies. He thought about the way his mood changed when he heard her voice. When he needed flights and engagements booked, she was right there.

She would come to all his exhibits when Michelle was too busy to attend. One thing he loved about Tracy, she never wanted anything from James, but his friendship; she never manipulated it. Who Tracy said she was, she was all the time. He liked that she didn't change her attitude. He watched Tracy as she slept on the plane, and he couldn't sleep.

James was in love. He wanted to tell Tracy, but she wouldn't believe him; he was about to get married a week ago. He had told her he was going to take his time. James wondered if she would be interested in him. The plane landed, and Tracy woke up.

James said, "Did you have a good nap?"

Tracy stretched and said, "It was the best nap ever." They got off the plane and went to the terminal to get their luggage. Tracy said, "If you ever have a trip like this again, I'm your girl." Those words gave James a thrill. He thought, *in more ways than you know.*

James said, "I'll keep you posted." He walked Tracy to her car. She kissed him on the cheek and drove off. James got into his and drove home. He kept thinking about Tracy and how she made him feel. He couldn't go home. He turned around and headed to her house, but Tracy wasn't there. He waited thirty minutes, she still wasn't home. He called her phone and it went to voicemail. He wondered where she could be.

He drove home and saw her car in his driveway.

Tracy said, "I waited for you; I have something to tell you."

"Can I tell you first?"

171

Tracy said, "Let's say it together." They both said, "I love you," with a surprised look on their faces. They hadn't expected to hear that, but it was said; it was confirmed; they were in love.

Tracy asked, "When did you fall in love with me?"

"I think I was always in love with you; the trip just confirmed it."

"I fell in love with you when I saw you painting; I thought if he can be that sensual with a paintbrush, I can imagine—" She then cleared her throat. "AHEM!"

James said, "Finish the sentence."

Tracy whispered, "Oh, how I want to—" She bit her lip. He kissed it. She says, "Mmm, I've been waiting and wanting this for a while."

James said, "Was it worth it?"

"More than you know."

"Tracy, I want to take care of you like my heart is saying to. I want to fulfill the desires of your heart. You don't ask me for anything and that makes me want to give you everything. Let me do that for you."

Tracy replied, "I will never stop you from doing something for me but don't feel like you are obligated to."

"That's why I crave you; you keep it so real."

"That's the only way to be." James kissed Tracy on the forehead. She said, "Mmm, that's another sensitive spot."

"And I plan on finding them all."

YOU'RE ON CANDACE'S CAMERA

Fasten your seat belt; that's what Laura heard over the speaker. The plane was running into some turbulence. Laura had caught the last flight out. The business meeting was over a day early. She couldn't wait to get home to her husband, Eric, to celebrate their wedding anniversary. She had been gone a week and wasn't due back until tomorrow. She had picked up a gift for him while she was out of town, so when she got home, she would have it all ready for him.

After the bumpy ride, they finally landed. She waited for her luggage to come down the conveyor belt. On the plane she was pondering if she would call or text him. Let him know she was coming home early. She decided not to, just surprise him. On her way home, she picked up a bottle of champagne to celebrate two occasions, her promotion and their anniversary. She had another surprise for him but that would wait until the appropriate time.

Laura pulled up in the driveway. She saw Eric's car there. He always parked the car in the garage. Why the sudden change? She was too tired to go through the garage. She parked her car in the front and went through the front door. She walked up the stairs to the bedroom and saw Eric sitting on the bed.

Eric said, "Hey, baby, you're home early."

Laura replied, "I know. The meeting was over early. I wanted to surprise you."

"You got me. I am surprised."

Laura heard the garage door opening. She was getting ready to go and see who it was when Eric grabbed her and kissed her.

Eric said, "Happy Anniversary, baby. That's my brother Devon. He came over earlier. Today we washed and waxed his car and waxed it in the garage. He's just leaving."

Laura thought it made sense. She always waxed her car in the garage.

Eric said, "So tell me about your trip."

Laura owned two bakeries. One in Virginia and one in the state she lived in, Texas. She catered a lot of events, so she was always out of town. When Eric was not busy, he traveled with her. Laura had owned the bakery in Texas for ten years. She just opened the other one two years ago. She catered an event for her best friend's wedding. She received positive feedback, so she decided to open one in that area, and it was as prosperous as the one in Texas. Her best friend, Joyce, managed the one in Virginia.

Laura said to Eric, "The trip was eventful. I interviewed two bakers and met with the bankers about the store next door." Laura was thinking about expanding her business in Virginia; she wanted to buy the available space next door. It'd been empty for some time, and since her business was prospering, she needed more space.

Eric said, "I'm proud of you. You said that you would make it work, and you did. I wish I had the faith you have. When you put your mind to it, it comes to pass."

"My father always told me nothing is given to you. You want it, work hard for it. Success only looks good when your hands are dirty. I'd rather have calloused hands to show I worked up a sweat to get it, than have clean hands and work towards nothing. You have to want something, not just anything."

Laura walked towards the bedroom window and saw the taillights of the car leaving the driveway. It was dark, but Laura was always on point about everything. She said to Eric, "Devon got a new car?"

"No, why do you ask?"

Laura said, "The taillights are different on this car."

"That's his girlfriend's car."

Laura responded, "Oh, I didn't know he had one."

Eric didn't respond. She turned around to see why, and he was sound asleep.

Laura thought, I guess we'll celebrate our anniversary another day. She grabbed the laundry basket, turned off the bedroom light, headed downstairs into the kitchen to put the champagne in the refrigerator, then out to the garage to do a load of laundry. She turned on the light in the garage, stepped down, and heard a crunch. She lifted her foot up and saw a diamond earring. She picked it up and touched her ears to make sure hers were intact.

They were. She knew it was not hers. She wanted to know whose ear it belonged to.

Laura never wanted to assume anything. She didn't want to assume, the earring she found, meant that Eric was cheating on her. Yet women's intuition always works. As much as she loved Eric, she wasn't putting up with his cheating ways. Laura could hold her own. She was very independent. Her daddy taught her that; he also told her never to settle for someone who can't make you stronger. You become your own rock, when others around you have sandy foundations.

Laura had always been faithful to Eric. Although he had marital affairs, she was true to her vows. His affairs yes, affairs, didn't start until Laura started going out of town. Eric was a police officer. He'd been on the force for twenty years. Eric and Laura met by accident; Eric ran into the back of Laura's car. They exchanged information. Due to the accident, Laura had a flat tire. The bumper hit the tire and flattened it. Her car had to be towed away.

Eric felt bad. He insisted he'd give her a ride home. Laura took a cab home. She didn't know Eric; although he said he was a police officer, she felt safer taking a cab home. Laura got the news her car was totaled, and she had to buy a new one. Eric received the news as well. He called Laura to apologize again for the accident.

Laura said, "Things happen for a reason."

Eric said, "And there's a reason why I'm calling. I feel bad about the accident. If you need to get a new car, I will make the down payment for you."

Laura said, "That's nice of you but my insurance took care of everything."

"Well, can I at least take you out to dinner?"

"Dinner sounds fine. Can I pick the restaurant?"

"Sure."

Laura made reservations. She sent Eric the information. Eric called Laura. He said, "You know this restaurant is in New York? I live in Texas!"

"I know it is. I'm here for an event, will be here for two weeks. If you want to take me out to dinner, you'll have to come to New York to do it."

Eric liked her feisty attitude. It rubbed him the right way. Laura was bold. Whatever she wanted, she got. She didn't demand anything, she just had standards. They stood like pillars, tall and strong. There was nothing weak about her.

Dinner at seven. That's the time Laura picked. She had arrived at 6:45pm. Another thing Eric was going to find about Laura was that she was prompt. If she said a certain time, she'd expect you to be there. That was a pet peeve of hers. She wouldn't be petting you if you didn't respect it. As Laura was being escorted to her table, Eric stood up and pulled out her seat.

Eric said, "Good evening, Laura."

"Good evening, Eric! It's so nice to see you made it. I'm impressed."

"I had some vacation time I hadn't used, so this was a perfect time to use it."

Laura asked, "Why are you interested in me?"

She wasted no time. She wanted facts now. Don't beat around the bush with this woman. Don't waste her time. Give her the information she's asking for. If you bore her, she will walk away and leave you right there.

Eric replied, "I just wanted to see you again."

"Okay you've seen me. Now what?"

"Since we're in a restaurant, let's order something to eat!"

Laura smiled. She liked how Eric could hold a candle to her. He wasn't backing down from her. Both were stubborn people, so they were just right for each other. They began dating after that, and two years later they married. Laura didn't start traveling until eight years after they were married. That's when she opened her second bakery. She had goals; wherever they led, she would follow. She was gone two weeks out of the month. Eric was okay with it at first. But then that day came.

A new officer started at the precinct. Eric was to train her. Her name was Theresa. She was pretty. Eric was drawn to her quickly. He flirted with her. She flirted back. He'd pocket his wedding ring every time he saw her. He didn't see one on hers, so he knew she wasn't married; well, he didn't ask either. A month in, they were intimate. Everywhere they could, they would. People on the force noticed the affair; it didn't take long for the news to get back to Laura. Most people adored her and had a lot respect for her.

Laura confronted Eric with the news, and he admitted it. She asked him why. He said he had needs, and since she was gone all the time, he needed them taken care of. Pitiful, she thought. It was the weakest thing she ever heard him say. It had to be more than that. They went to counseling to work things out.

That had been a while ago. Now Laura was getting tired of the marriage. She didn't trust him after the affair. She didn't feel his love. She didn't feel a lot of things. She had so much invested in her marriage, though; for her to make a change, she needed proof he was cheating. She needed to find out whose earring this was.

Laura went back up to the bedroom. She didn't say anything to Eric about what she found in the garage. Her mind wandered all night about that earring. Why was it in her garage? She didn't allow any women in her house. Her best friend was in Virginia; she didn't have any sisters. She was going to find out because that earring was trespassing on her premises. She needed to find the owner.

In the morning, Eric got dressed for work. Laura was going into the bakery later. She got a text about a client who wanted some cakes and cupcakes done for an event. Eric kissed Laura goodbye, and he headed out.

Laura called the client. She said, "Hello, may I speak to Candace?"

Candace replied, "Speaking!"

Laura replied, "I received your information about your order. Did you have a particular way you wanted your cakes and cupcakes done?"

Candace said, "I've seen some of your cakes. I'd like to see some more designs if it's no problem?"

"No problem at all. I can meet you at your house in about an hour."

"That's fine. I live right across the street."

"Okay, I will see you then."

Laura grabbed some of her albums, got dressed and walked across the street to Candace's house. She rang the doorbell. Candace answered. Laura introduced herself, and Candace gestured for her to come in. Candace asked, "Would you like something to drink?"

Laura replied, "Water would be fine."

Candace went to get Laura a bottle of water. Laura opened her collection of photos to show Candace when she returned. Candace handed the water to Laura, and she said thank you. Laura said, "So what's the occasion you need the cakes for? I can show you many designs."

Candace replied, "I'm not having an event."

Laura looked puzzled. She said, "Then why did you ask for my services?"

"Because I have something to show you. Wait right here!"

Candace went upstairs to grab her laptop. When she returned, Laura had a look of concern on her face. Candace said, "Ms.

Laura, I know you're out of town a lot. I also know that you don't allow anyone over to your house. You are a very private person and I know you keep to yourself. I've noticed when you are out of town, there is a lot of activity that goes on over there."

Laura said, "What do you mean, a lot of activity?"

Candace opened her laptop. She rewound the tape from her outside cameras to last week when Laura was out of town. Candace showed Laura what activity was going on: a car going up her driveway, a lady getting out of it, Eric coming out of the house and greeting her with a kiss that only Laura should be getting. Eric pressed the key for the garage door to open, the woman drove her car in it. Laura was hurt, but not surprised. Candace showed her the activity for the whole week she was out of town.

Then Laura saw the next video. It showed the night she came home. Eric's car was parked outside, and Laura went in the house. Ten minutes later she saw a car coming out of her garage and driving down the driveway. Laura told Candace to pause it. She said, "Can you zoom in on the driver?"

Candace said, "Yes, ma'am!"

Laura looked closely at the driver. It was Theresa. Laura said, "So that's who was leaving my house when I was upstairs talking to Eric. He told me it was his brother Devon." Laura then asked Candace, "Why are you showing me this?"

Candace pulled out a picture of a little girl. "This is my daughter, Deja; she's five years old. I haven't done a DNA test yet, but I know it's his daughter. I met Eric six years ago at a friend's party. We messed around for a while. When I told him I was pregnant, he told me to get an abortion. I told him no, but he gave me money to have one. I took the money and moved. When I moved into this house two years ago, I was shocked and scared that he lived right across from me. So, I had cameras installed and I sent a link to my brother. If anything happened to me, he had proof that someone came into my house."

Laura sat there with her mouth wide open in disbelief. Candace said, "I've wanted to talk you for some time. I didn't know how to approach you. When I saw that he was up to his old tricks again, disrespecting you, I had to do something. When I saw your bakery, I wrote down your number. The only way I could get you to come over was to act like I wanted to put in an order. I didn't want to talk on the phone, plus I didn't know when he would be home. I didn't want to talk while he was home.

"Ms. Laura, I'm so sorry, you don't deserve this. I don't know you personally, but I feel that you deserve better than what you are getting now."

"Does he know you live across the street?"

"I don't think so. If I need to leave out of the house I go out the back door. He doesn't know I had my baby; he hasn't seen me in five years. I'm scared, Ms. Laura. I'm looking for a new place to live." Laura hugged Candace, and Candace cried.

Laura said, "I want to share something with you, as you have shared with me. I can't have children. I had to have an emergency hysterectomy because of the tumors. Meeting you was not an accident; it was on purpose for more reasons than you know. Are you working? How are you supporting Deja?"

Candace said, "I'm not working right now. My parents provide for me, but I'd like to have my own."

Laura asked, "What do you like to do"?

"I like to cook and bake!"

"Bake what?"

"I dib and dab. I like to make cookies and all sorts of things."

Laura said, "Can I ask how old you are?"

"I'm twenty-eight!"

"You ever moved out of town before?"

Candace said, "I wanted to move back to Virginia where my mom and dad are. Ms. Laura, you are so calm; you don't seem upset."

"If you only knew what I've been through."

Just then Deja came down the steps from taking her nap. She walked over to Candace. "Mommy, I'm hungry."

Candace introduced Deja to Laura. Laura looked at Deja and saw that she was Eric's daughter; she looked just like him. Laura picked Deja up and hugged her. Candace's eyes welled up in tears. Laura rocked Deja as if she was putting her to sleep. Deja took to Laura instantly. As Laura was with Deja, Candace went to fix her something to eat. Laura sung Deja a lullaby. Deja hugged Laura like a teddy bear.

Laura looked at her watch. She had been at Candace's house for four hours. Laura carried Deja into the kitchen where her mother was. She said to Candace, "I have to go now. I will be in touch with you."

"Ms. Laura are you going to be alright?" Candace asked.

"I'm stronger than I look." She kissed Deja on the cheek and left.

Laura went home to get her car, went out to run a few errands, and called Devon.

Laura said, "Hello, Devon, how are you?"

"Sis-in-law, I'm doing fine how's the bakery in Virginia doing?"

"It's prospering."

"That's awesome. So, what's up?"

"When was the last time you talked with Eric?"

"I talked to him about a month ago."

"So, you weren't over to my house last night?"

Devon said, "No, I'm out of town. I won't be back until Saturday."

"Okay, I thank you for this information."

"He put my name in a lie again, didn't he?"

"You know your brother. Hugs and kisses."

Devon replied, "Kisses and hugs. Talk with you later."

Laura made a few more calls, stopped by the store to pick up some things for dinner, and headed home. Eric came home twenty minutes later. He said hello.

Laura responded, "Hey, there."

Eric said, "That was short."

"I have some things on my mind."

"You care to share?"

"No, I just have an emergency business meeting. I need to catch a flight out tomorrow. I'll return Sunday."

Eric said, "But you just got back in town."

"Business is business."

After dinner was done, Laura went upstairs to pack her suitcase. She wanted to say so much to Eric, but the timing wasn't right. She said, "I picked up some new toothbrushes, just the kind you like."

Eric said, "Thank you!"

Morning came, Eric got dressed for work. He asked Laura what time her flight was. She said later this morning, and he said to call him when she landed. Laura waited for Eric's car to go down the driveway. She made a call while she waited. Twenty minutes after he left, she did.

Candace's garage door opened. Laura drove her car in it, and the garage door closed. Laura grabbed her suitcase and went into Candace's kitchen.

Candace said, "Ms. Laura, let me show you to your room."

Candace took Laura up to the guest room, and Laura unpacked her bag. She handed Candace a sandwich bag with Eric's toothbrush in it. Laura said, "I made you an appointment tomorrow at 8:00 am to take the DNA test; it's already paid for. We are going to get to the bottom of this." Candace thanked Laura. Deja came in the room. Laura said, "Hey, Deja, how are you?

Deja said, "Hi, Ms. Laura! I'm fine."

Laura picked up Deja and gave her a big kiss. Later that day they were in the kitchen cooking. Candace had her laptop in the kitchen, so she could see what went on in front of the house. Laura looked at the laptop and saw a car pulling up in the driveway. It wasn't Eric's car; it was Theresa's. Theresa hit the garage door opener and went into the garage.

Laura said, "Eric must have given her the key today. We only have two, and he used his yesterday." Laura wasn't upset; her plan was coming together. She waited to see him come home. Thirty minutes later, he parked his car in the driveway.

Laura saw this activity go on for two days. On the third day there was going to be a surprise. That morning Candace made breakfast and called Laura and Deja down to eat. Laura and Deja came down. Laura said, "Ms. Deja slept in my bed last night. She snuck in my bed and just laid her pretty head on my pillow."

Deja said, "I love Ms. Laura. She's fun."

Laura said, "I love you too, Deja."

Candace had seen the mail come in and she went to go grab it. It was the results for the DNA test, saying that there was a 99.9 percent chance Eric Long was the father of Deja Johnson. Candace showed Laura the results. Laura said to Candace, "We have work to do tomorrow."

The next day Laura waited for Eric to leave. As soon as he left, Laura went over to the house, and the locksmith met her there thirty minutes later. She changed all the locks on the house, changed the garage door opener. It was all done in a matter of four hours. Laura went back over to Candace's house and waited for Eric to get home. Like clockwork, Theresa pulled up in the driveway. She sat there for about five minutes, then she got out the car, called someone on her cell phone and waited. Ten minutes later, Eric drove up. She handed him the garage opener, but the garage didn't open. Eric went to the front door and his key didn't work. He went around the back door, to no avail. His keys didn't work.

Eric came back to Theresa. He said, "I don't know what's going on. My wife is out of town. I don't know what happened; everything was working this morning." As he was talking, Laura walked up the driveway. The look on Eric and Theresa's faces were priceless. Laura walked up to Theresa and looked at her ears; one diamond earring was missing. Laura said, "I believe this cubic belongs to you." She handed it to Theresa.

She walked over to Eric and handed him an envelope, holding her hand up to shut off his protests about how Theresa coming over wasn't what it seemed. "You may want to look at this." He opened the envelope and saw the DNA results along with divorce papers. Laura said to Eric, "I ran into a young lady by the name of Candace. Does that name sound familiar to you, Eric?" He nodded with a look of dread on his face. "I had an interesting conversation with her. As we were conversing, I had a chance to meet her daughter, your daughter, Eric. She looks just like you. As you can see, the DNA results confirm you are the father.

187

"Deja is your daughter's name. She is now five years old. You are going to pay back child support; yes, my lawyer is helping me with that as well. I had news to tell you when I came home that night, but we were interrupted by the garage door opening when Theresa was leaving. Yes, Eric, it wasn't Devon leaving that night. I confirmed that with him, plus I have her leaving on video. I have all that I need and so does my lawyer.

"As much as I have been good to you, Eric, you've shown me that, that's not what you want. You don't want a good woman, so I'm going to give you what you do deserve: a divorce. I changed all the locks and garage door opener this morning. my lawyer has all the videos of, *YOU,* Ms. Theresa, entering my house. I am selling this property. You two have trespassing warrants against you; I suggest you step off my property. But before you both leave, turn around and Smile. You're on Candace's Camera."

A month went by. Laura had finished packing up the moving truck. Her house was on the market and sold within two weeks. She packed up Eric's clothes and left them by the garage, told him to pick them up before trash day, which would be tomorrow. Laura saw Deja running up to her, and Laura picked her up.

Deja said, "Hello, Ms. Laura!"

Laura said, "Hey, Pumpkin, you all ready to go?"

"Yes, ma'am, I am!"

Laura carried Deja to the truck and handed her to Candace. Candace put Deja in her car seat and fastened her up. Laura was moving to Virginia to oversee the renovation; she was taking Candace and Deja with her and they would stay with her. Candace was a good baker after all. She'd be a baker in the store Joyce managed. Laura and Candace's parents would take turns babysitting Deja when she got out of kindergarten school. Candace was receiving child support for Deja, and Laura started a trust fund for her as well. Devon was managing the bakery in Texas. Candace's cameras were installed at their new place. Smile, you might be on them too……

"Bang, bang, bang." Courtney banged on her sister Tina's car window; Tina didn't respond. "Bang, bang, bang, Tina, Tina!" No response. Courtney said to Donovan, "Get a brick, bust the window."

"Bang, bang, bang. Tina, Tina," Courtney cried. Donovan smashed the passenger window and unlocked the door. Courtney opened the door, pulled Tina from the car, removed the earbuds from her ears and saw an empty bottle of pills on the floor. She checked Tina's pulse. She had one—light, but she had one.

Courtney told Donovan call 911. "Tina, wake up, wake up, please wake up. He's not worth it; he's not worth it, wake up!" No response. Courtney started rocking her. "Please wake up, please, Tina, wake up." The ambulance arrived. Courtney grabbed the empty bottle of pills and gave it to the paramedic. Courtney said, "I think she overdosed." The ambulance rushed Tina to the hospital; Courtney and Donovan rode behind ambulance. When they arrived, Donovan and Courtney waited outside the emergency room.

The nurse started pumping Tina's stomach, the heart rate monitors slowly going up and down. Courtney looked through the glass. She saw them working on Tina, then the heart monitor flat lined. Courtney screamed. Donovan came to see what was wrong. "She's dead, Donovan, Tina's gone, our sister is dead!" Courtney screamed, and they hugged, trying to console each other. Courtney called their parents to give them the news. Their parents lived in Atlanta, Ga; Tina, Donovan and Courtney lived in Virginia. They all went to college there and had decided to stay.

Courtney was the eldest; Tina was the middle child, and Donovan the youngest. They were raised in Atlanta; after Tina and Donovan finished high school, their parents wanted them all to go to the same college they had, so they moved to Virginia with Courtney, so she could look after them. Tina had moved to Virginia five years ago. She majored in business. She wanted to be a financial analyst. She was always good with numbers; math was her gift, even as a child. Her dad noticed that gift early. She wanted to please her parents too; she was a Daddy's girl. She could get away with murder, and her dad would hide the body.

Tina was special and gifted; that's what made her different. She fell in love with her study partner, Lewis. They had started school around the same time. He was from South Carolina. They met in class accidentally; she sat in a seat, pulled out her books, and waited for the teacher to begin. Lewis walked up to her and said, "Excuse me, you're sitting in my chair!"

With humor, Tina looked all around the seat, lifted it up, and said to him, "I don't see your name on it, but my butt is in it for now. I can warm it up for you, and if you want it after class is over, I will gladly give to you."

Lewis liked her humor. She was sarcastic, quick and to the point; she was a sharpshooter; she'd hit the target right on the

191

bullseye. Tina's aura filled the room; you knew she was there. She'd walk in the room and you would hear this uproar; people were glad to see her. You thought she was famous. She was normal, but people made her feel famous. She didn't do anything different; she didn't bring attention to herself, her personality did it for her.

Tina was like a magnet; people were drawn to her. She was an encourager, and she loved people. The right words must have been written on her tongue, and she would speak them at the right time, not missing a beat. Tina was going somewhere, and her family was backing her up every step of the way. Tina and Lewis came from similar backgrounds. They had a lot to talk about. Lewis came to Virginia on a basketball scholarship, and so did Tina. She loved basketball. She started playing in middle school. She was a point guard; she glided on the court with the ball like she was ice skating. She was poetry in motion; she looked like a ballerina leaping in the air. She dominated the court. She was a team player, but when it was time to score, Tina put herself in position and made it happen.

Tina and Lewis would play one on one at times. They'd draw a crowd. She played like there was a trophy to gain, and she was claiming it at the end of the game. She played street ball, no refs, so if she fouled, couldn't no one call it. It was rough, but she was tough. Lewis liked that about her. She was a tomboy on the court, but a lady when she walked off it. They liked each other's company, which they noticed when they were studying for exams.

Tina had an apartment not too far from campus. Lewis would come over and study.

One night, studying, Lewis said. "I like your style."

Tina replied, "What does that mean?"

"I like you as a person!"

"Why didn't you say that in the first place?"

"I like you as a person, Tina. Is that better?" Lewis replied.

"Yes, I understand that," Tina said.

"We spend a lot of time together. I'd like to study you instead of studying for these exams."

Tina turned on the bright light. She said, "Interrogate me; would you like to know where I was last night?"

Lewis laughed. "No, I don't want to know that." He whispered, "I'd like to know where you been all my life?" He kissed Tina unexpectedly; she kissed him like she expected to.

Tina said, "So what does this mean?"

Lewis replied, "It means I want to kiss these lips for a while."

"I'd like that." Tina and Lewis dated throughout college. After graduation, they moved in together. They both had promising jobs. Their future seemed set in stone, and that's what Tina wanted, a rock on her finger. Lewis liked the relationship the way it was. Tina wanted more. They argued about it. She knew her worth, and he already downgraded it. The arguments were so heated, Tina decided to move out. The situation was too complicated to continue. She moved in with Courtney until things calmed down. Courtney told Tina not to go back to him, no matter what.

Tina knew in her heart that Lewis would never marry her; she had already given him the husband treatment before the ring. Every ounce of her love was in Lewis. They talked every now and then, and she never brought up marriage again. When she didn't, the conversation went smoothly. Tina would ask at times when she would see him again. We will schedule something would always be his response. Lewis had been real busy with his promotion, and he really didn't have time for a social life.

Lewis knew how Tina felt about him; he also knew that she would do anything for him. He was selfish. She was burnt out, but she still gave. Lewis milked her heart like it was a cow. She poured into him, and he wasn't pouring back into her. She'd tell him how handsome he was, stroke his ego for days; he would never have anything to say back to her. He would leave her panting like someone thirsting for water, and he would leave her right there, not quenching anything, not even a drop.

Tina only wanted a compliment. He wouldn't form his mouth to give her one. She almost had to beg for his attention. She was hurt; he was draining her to the point she didn't have anything else to say. Instead of talking, she started sending gifts, hoping that would change his thinking. She sent chocolate-covered strawberries to his job, a thinking-of-you gesture. After the delivery was confirmed, Tina went by his workplace to take him out to lunch. She walked up to his office and saw the strawberries on his desk. He had one in his hand, feeding it to a young lady sitting on his desk.

Lewis saw Tina, and he didn't budge. She stood there, devastated, and she walked out. She waited in her car to see if he would come out, but he never did. She drove home and cried out to Courtney. Courtney asked, "Why do you put yourself through this? You believe in his lies; you trust what he says. He's showing you who he is; he's playing mind games with you. The more he thinks you believe what he says, the more he'll keep telling you. He can hear it in your voice that you believe him, that's why he keeps telling you. After he gets off the phone with you, he's probably saying that girl is so naïve. You're probably not the only one he's doing this to. Even if he's doing this to someone else, don't be a part of that number. Tina, you are too beautiful to be tied up in this. If he's not reaching out to you, why waste your time with him? He obviously doesn't care about your feelings. He doesn't call you up to see how your day is going. He doesn't think you're important to him. If he was thinking about you, he'd call you. Why do you have to be the first one to do everything? You're worth so much, Tina. Until you see that, he will always treat you like this."

Tina said in a small voice, "He would always say, one day I'll show you."

Courtney replied, "One day you'll see, one day, one day. That day is never coming, Tina. He showed you today. Stop wanting someone that doesn't want you. He doesn't care. Live your life; he's living his." Tina cried in Courtney's arms.

Tina said, "I should've paid attention to a dream I had some years ago."

Courtney replied, "What dream?"

Tina said, "In my dream; I went to his house. In front of the house was a high barbed wired gate. Beyond the gate was a bunch of garbage, it was all this clutter. If I had tried to climb the gate I would've injured myself, so I called Lewis to come to the gate to let me in. He opened the door and stood in the doorway. He didn't move the clutter to try to get to me; he just stood there. He wanted to see if I would climb that gate to get to him. I would've hurt myself, Courtney, trying to get to him. There was a barricade between him and me. I stood there and cried; he smiled at me and went back in the house. It was just a dream, Courtney, but it seemed so real, and now the very same thing I saw in my dream is happening."

Tina's heart was broken. She loved a man who didn't love her back; he fooled her with his words and now her heart grieved with his lies. She was distraught. She said, "Why did I let him do this to me?"

Courtney said, "He didn't do that to you; you did that to yourself. Never give someone that much control over your heart and emotions." Courtney called Donovan, told him to come over to help her with Tina. Tina went to go get a glass of wine and sat on the couch. She was scrolling through her phone. She got a text message from her girlfriend that Lewis had gotten engaged and his girlfriend was expecting. Tina threw the glass up against the wall and screamed, screamed, screamed. Courtney said, "What's wrong?" Just then Donovan knocked on the door. Courtney answered it and Tina stormed past them. Donovan tried to grab Tina, but she snatched herself away from him.

She said, "Leave me alone!"

Donovan asked Courtney, "What's wrong?"

"Tina looked at her phone and lost it. Let her calm down. Help me clean up this mess." He went in and saw the splatter on the wall.

"What happened?" Donovan asked.

"She threw the glass of wine and started crying."

Donovan asked, "What happened before that?"

"She was crying about Lewis."

"That jerk!" Donovan replied. I told her to leave him alone, he wasn't any good for her. She said she was in love with him. I said yes, but he's not in love with you; there's a difference. Love somebody that's going to love you back." Donovan told Courtney he was with Tina one day and he saw some pills in her purse. "I asked her what they were for.

"Tina replied, 'For pain.' I asked her, 'Pain for what?' She said, 'For my heart.' So, I asked her, 'What's wrong with your heart?' and she said, 'Nothing right now.'

"It was really weird," Donovan said.

An hour went by. Tina hadn't come back home. Courtney started to get worried. She called Tina's phone and it went straight to voicemail.

Courtney said, "Let me walk outside and see if I see her."

"I'll stay here in case she comes back or calls." Courtney walked outside. She didn't see Tina's car, so she walked across the street to the park. She saw a car with the lights on; it looked like Tina's car. She ran over to it and started banging on the window. She called Donovan and told him to come across the street. On the way to the hospital, Courtney was looking through Tina's phone. She had sent a message to Lewis—*this is my last goodbye to you. You won't hear from me anymore.* There was no return text from him.

After Courtney and Donovan left the hospital, Courtney went to get Tina's car to put it in the garage. Donovan taped the broken window. Courtney sat in Tina's car and cried. Courtney was trying to make sense of all this and couldn't. She just kept crying. She grabbed Tina's purse, just to hold something of hers. Sticking out of the purse was a letter; Courtney saw her name on it. She opened it.

"Dear Courtney, I am gone now. I'm sorry I didn't say goodbye to you. I love you so much. Tell Mommy and Daddy I love them with all my heart. I couldn't live in this world knowing I couldn't be loved. Lewis is not allowed to come to my funeral. If he couldn't see me while I was alive, he can't see me now that I'm gone. Promise me that. I want to go back home with Mommy and Daddy. I don't want him to visit my grave. I want to be Far Away from him, as he chose to be with me. I love you, Courtney. I'll love you always."

Courtney cried, cried, cried. Donovan came to the car. Courtney showed him the letter. He closed his eyes and cried out loud. Courtney had Tina's earbuds. She wanted to know what she was listening to before she died. "If you only knew" was her favorite song; it expressed how she felt about Lewis.

Courtney locked Tina's car up and left for the airport to go pick up their parents. They then drove to the hospital to see Tina. They walked in the room, and she lay there peacefully. Courtney said, "She's at peace now." Courtney's mom and dad just looked at Tina and consoled each other with hugs and tears. Courtney stared at Tina; she couldn't take her eyes off her. Courtney said, "I was supposed to protect you, and I failed. I am so sorry, Tina. You rest now. No one can ever hurt you again."

The word of Tina's death spread like wildfire. Lewis came to Courtney's house. Donovan grabbed Lewis by the throat and choked him. Courtney broke it up. "He's not worth it," Courtney said. And to Lewis, "You have no right to be here."

Lewis responded, "I wanted to pay my respects."

"You came to pay your respect to a person you disrespected! Leave please, don't ever come back to my house again. Her wishes were that you do not come to her funeral; we will see to it that it happens. I hope I never see you again, Lewis. You were the cause of her pain, and I don't want to rehearse this pain I'm feeling again, so I pray this is the last time I see you. Please leave now." Lewis left, and Donovan slammed the door behind him.

A week later Tina's funeral was held. She knew many people and they loved her. They paid their respects with as much love as she gave to them. Donovan made sure Lewis did not attend; he stood outside to make sure he didn't approach the church steps. Courtney gave the eulogy. She expressed how much spunk Tina had, how much joy and love she gave. She was the best little sister, and she couldn't be replaced. She was one of a kind and would always be remembered.

Courtney said, "You are too far away that I can't see you, too Far Away that I can't talk to you, too far away that I can't spend time with you, but I will hold you close to me in my heart. Goodbye, Tina." Tina's body was flown back to Atlanta with her parents. Courtney kept Tina's car, got the window fixed, and kept her car in the garage."

Courtney went into Tina's room and sat on the edge of her bed. She rocked back and forth with Tina's picture in her hand. "I will miss you so much, Tina. I wish I had known how much pain you were in. I forgive myself for not paying attention to you. Now you're gone, so far away from me...but you will always be in my heart. ALWAYS."

FORGIVE THEM

Searching into the deep core of the heart, I was handed the keys to unlock the Chest of Mysteries. While the owner of the heart lay panting in despair, he allowed me to open each chamber of his heart and read every word of his pain. As I read, I wept, for he held onto this pain for so long, it was buried like lost treasure in the ocean.

There were layers of pain; I saw names in alphabetical order. Times and dates were etched next to them. For every hurt, abuse, misuse someone did to him, he held onto their names. He wrapped chains around them; he was holding them hostage. As I looked at his face, I could see his anger. The more he inhaled, the tighter the chains became around the names. I tried touching the chains, and they pricked me like thorns.

I stepped back to the see the heart from a distance. The tighter the chains became, the more it bled. I saw drops of blood every time he inhaled. I stepped closer, and every time he took a breath, the thorns on the chains cut into his heart. I could see the venom of anger going through the ventricles of his heart. It was black; the anger was poison. The heart that used to be red became black like a smoker's lungs. I looked into the owner's eyes, and they looked like a black hole, no life.

This soul was dying, panting like he was suffocating, trying to catch his last breath. How could I help him? How could I save him? His eyes were growing dimmer, like the sun setting; the sockets of his eyes were getting darker. I screamed out, "I need you to live and not die!" I thought why is he holding these names hostage? In my spirit I heard, *he needs to forgive them.* Quickly, I whispered in his ear. *Forgive them; set them free.*

I heard him gasp like he had taken his last breath. His breathing became normal. I looked into his eyes, and I saw the light of day. I looked at his heart. The chains fell on the ground. Every name he had held hostage was set free like a caged bird. I looked into the eyes of life and said you have set them free; now be free and live.

UNEXPECTED APPRECIATION

Ring, ring, ring. "Thank you for calling Jazz Construction; can you hold? Thank you for calling Jazz Construction; can you hold?" Ring, ring, ring! Grand opening day and the phones were ringing off the hook. Jasmine had just opened her construction company with her husband, Tony, and they'd named it Jazz, short for Jasmine. She was an architect; Tony worked construction, so they decided to open their own business. Since they had a lot of clientele from previous businesses, their first day, business skyrocketed. All kinds of proposals were coming in. They hadn't thought their phones would be that busy.

Jasmine and Tony were answering the phones, and while doing so, they were running out of items. *I need paper, I need a pen, my pencil broke.* It was too funny – busy, busy, busy; all the lines were blinking. Jazz said, "Baby, we need some more people. I know we prayed for our business to prosper, but I didn't know it was going to be like this on the first day." Tony agreed. After the day slowed down, Jazz began making calls of her own. She needed help quickly, so she called her cousin Lela.

Lela was looking for a job, so she could save up and buy a car. She would be perfect for the job; she was a talker, she liked to be busy. This would give her something to do and a way to earn money. Ring, ring. "Hello, Lela?" Jasmine said.

203

Lela replied, "Yes."

"This is Jasmine. How are you?"

"I'm fine. Hey, congratulations on your grand opening; how is it going for the first day?"

Jasmine laughed and said, "It's funny you should ask that; my phone has been ringing off the hook."

"Well, that's a good thing, right?" Lela replied.

Jasmine replied, "Yes, it's awesome. Tony and I have a lot of work to do. I have to get proposals in the mail, draw up some designs, and I was wondering."

"Say no more," Lela replied. "I'll come and help you guys out."

"You were always a mind reader."

Lela replied, "Yeah, and I can read between lines very well too." They both laughed.

Jasmine said, "Tomorrow we open at 9:00 am."

Lela replied. "I'll be there at 8:45." Jasmine knew she could depend on Lela; she was always on time. That was a pet peeve of Lela's. She didn't waste her time or anybody else's. for a young woman, Lela had a lot of old soul skills. She didn't club, so hanging out wasn't her thing. She liked to be around older people between ages thirty and forty. She had been raised with good values; she wasn't a sassy mouth, but very mature for her age.

Lela liked to work. She had started working at the age of fifteen, in the summertime. She liked this one daycare that she worked at very much, and they liked her as well. Every summer, they would ask her to come back and work. She loved kids. She didn't have any of her own. Lela was smart; some girls her age already had one. Lela wanted to get married and have children, like her mother and father had. She had been raised in a two-parent home, and her parents were still married, celebrating thirty years next year.

Lela was a daddy's girl. He taught her all the basics, about the birds and bees, snakes and dogs too. "Men can be one of those," he said. "Wait for one who will value you. Never give your heart to someone that's not going to give you theirs. You want to know how a man is supposed to treat a woman, ask your mother." Lela was equipped with a lot of knowledge during her young years, and she never forgot them because her daddy wouldn't let her.

Lela showed up for work at 8:30. She did that, so she could learn her job and do it professionally. She wanted to know what to say, how to put calls on hold and transfer. She was taking notes. She wanted to make a good impression on her cousins. She was dependable, and she wanted it to stay that way. At 9:00 am, the phones started ringing.

"Thank you for calling Jazz Construction, this is Lela speaking; can you hold please?" Lela did that with eight calls, and within two minutes she had answered every one of them, taken down information, details and all. At 9:15 am, she was off the phone. She took all the information to Jasmine and ran back to her seat. The phones started up again, and she ran through her spiel.

Ring, ring, ring; hold, hold, hold. She was a pro at this; you would think she had eight arms. She never missed a beat.

Jasmine stood there and watched her work. She was impressed. When Lela got off the phone, Jasmine said, "How would you like a permanent position?"

"I would like that. You sure you don't want to hire someone else?"

Jasmine replied, "Tony and I couldn't handle the phones like you did; I don't think I need to hire anyone else."

"What's the salary like? We never did talk about that."

Jasmine said, "I know. I wanted to see how your first day would go. Since business is off to a good start, how does fifteen an hour sound?"

"Sounds like I'll be back here on Monday. Let me call my daddy and tell him the good news. She called him. "Daddy, Daddy, Jasmine wants to hire me permanently."

Her father replied, "That's good. If you save your money for three months, I'll help you get a car."

"Bet, I'll do just that." Lela could have had a car by now; her father would've gotten it for her. Lela preferred to work for what she wanted, but he was her backup if she needed to get anything. Her lunch break was over, and she went back to her desk. No calls. Fifteen minutes went by, still no calls. As soon as she got up to ask Jasmine something, the phone rang. Lela said, "Thank you for calling Jazz Construction, this is Lela. How can I help you?"

The voice said, "I'd like to book my hotel for next Friday!"

"I'm sorry, you have the wrong number."

The voice replied, "Is this 203 454 6787?"

Lela replied, "Yes, this is the number. You may have written the number down wrong."

"I apologize."

"That's okay." She hung up the phone. The phones were busy for the rest of the day. It was five o' clock, and Lela was ready to call it quits. She had liked her first day. She said good night to Jazz and Tony and headed over to her parents' house before going home. Lela has a condo that her parents bought her for graduation. She only paid for electric and cable; you could say she had two homes since she still had a key to their house.

She walked in. "Mommy, Daddy, where are you?"

"We're in the kitchen, Lela," they replied. She walked in, gave her dad a kiss on the cheek, and her mom a bear hug. Her mom said, "Tell me how your first day was."

"It was super busy, but I managed it."

"Your daddy said Jasmine is hiring you permanently; that is awesome!"

"Yes, I'm so excited."

Her daddy said, "Well, I have a proposition for you."

"Yes, Daddy, what is it?" Lela said.

"Let me buy you your car, and you just pay me monthly for it," he replied.

"Daddy! Like buy my car with cash?"

He replied, "Yes."

Lela said, "Okay, I don't want any 1960 car; I'm too cute to drive a Pinto."

Her daddy laughed and said, "Whatever year you want, you can get it."

"I want a Mercedes!"

"I said year, not brand."

Lela laughed and said, "What's for dinner?"

Her mother replied, "Spaghetti, you hungry?"

"I'm starving." Her mom fixed her a plate with some garlic bread. When Lela was finished and full, she said, "I'm tired. I'm about to go give my pillow some head."

Her mom and dad at the same time said, "Lela, you better watch your mouth."

Lela replied, "What? Give my pillow some head means lay my head on the pillow like I'm going to sleep." Mom gave Lela a look like *don't say that again.* She kissed them both goodnight. Although she had her own place, she still had a room there, and since they were going shopping for a car tomorrow, there was no point in going home. Up to her room she went. Her head hit that pillow so hard it was a TKO on contact.

In the morning, Lela's cell phone rang; it was Jasmine. "Hey, Jazz, what's going on?"

Jazz replied, "I have a message for you."

"From whom?"

"Someone called and left a message about booking a hotel."

Lela replied, "Yes, I remember. I told him he had the wrong number."

"He did mention your name."

"Well, of course, I said my name when I answered the phone. I told him he had the wrong number."

"Well, it could've been the wrong number, but I think it's the right man."

"Oh, really?"

"I think he knows you."

"How do you figure that?"

"Because he's standing in my office; asking for you," Jazz replied.

"Does he have you at gunpoint?"

Jasmine laughed. "No, but I think you should come down to the office."

Lela replied, "It's my day off."

"I think it will be worth coming in."

"Okay, but I'm bringing my daddy with me."

"I think your daddy will approve of him."

"Approve of what? I don't even know who he is."

"You'll know him when you get here."

Lela said, "Okay." She hung up the phone and told her father before they went to look for a car, she had to go by the office and see Jasmine. Her father agreed. They arrived, and Lela asked, "Okay, what is this about?" Out walked Timothy. Lela knew exactly who he was. They used to work at the same daycare every summer. They had crushes on each other, puppy love moments. He would always say she was his girlfriend, and she'd say the same thing, but it was nothing serious.

Lela said, "Hello, Timothy, it's been a while." She walked up to him and gave him a hug. "So, what are you up to?"

Timothy replied, "Oh nothing. I work across the street. When I saw you yesterday, I wrote down the number on the business window where you work. I wanted to hear your voice, so I called acting like I was booking a room at a hotel."

Lela's father cleared his throat. "Ahem."

"Oh, Timothy let me introduce you to my father. Daddy, this is Timothy; Timothy, this is my Daddy, Mr. Daniels." They shook hands.

"Nice to meet you, sir."

Daddy said, "Likewise."

Lela asked Timothy, "So is there a reason you wanted to see me?"

Timothy replied, "Yes, I wanted to know if you were single." Lela's father cleared his throat again. "No disrespect, Mr. Daniels," Timothy said. "I have respect for your daughter; she has always been a lady to me. I'm a youth pastor at the church we used to work at during the summer."

"Oh, wow, that's awesome!" replied Lela.

"Yes, I love kids, so I knew that was my calling, to minister to the youth. The kids that we used to watch, I minister to now. It's fun. You should come by the church sometime. I bet they still remember you," Timothy said.

"I would like that. It's been years since I've seen them. You really think they still remember me? They were so little."

"Not that little. Come by this Sunday; it's youth Sunday."

Lela said, "I have no plans, so I will definitely make it." Lela and Timothy exchanged numbers; Mr. Daniels shook Timothy's hand, and what a hand grip he gave him.

Timothy said, "It was nice meeting you Mr. Daniels. If you're ever in the market for a car, here's my card."

Mr. Daniels replied, "Can we get your employee discount?"

"Who's looking for a car?"

"We are for Lela."

Timothy replied, "If she was my wife, she could get it."

Mr. Daniels replied, "We can do the ceremony right now!"

"Daddy!"

"I'm just kidding."

Timothy said, "So was I. I'm not working today, but I can take you over and show you some selections."

"If you're not going to get the sale, then I'd rather not do it today."

Timothy replied, "We are only looking."

"But what if I want it now?"

Timothy said, "Don't worry about it, I can still write it up."

Mr. Daniels asked, "What dealership do you work for?"

"Mercedes Benz."

Lela smiled; Mr. Daniels grunted. Lela asked Timothy, "What do you drive?"

"A 2018 Mercedes E Class, I just got it about two weeks ago; that new car smell is still lingering."

Lela replied, "Yes, I like that smell."

Timothy said, "Well, let's check some out then." They walked across the street. Timothy opened the door, they walked in, and Lela's eyes lit up like Christmas, Mr. Daniels looking like the Grinch who's getting ready to steal it.

Lela said, "Fix your face, Daddy, we're only looking."

"Okay, okay, okay." Lela looked around with her father following. She looked at a c-class coupe; it looked like a black diamond cut real nice. She sat in it, and the seats hugged her like a man's arms. She was snuggled in it. She caressed the steering wheel while her body was resting comfortably in the seat. She leaned her head back, closed her eyes, and gently touched the pedals, making sure the seat was adjusted correctly to reach them.

She opened the door and said, "Daddy..."

"I know; this is what you want."

Lela replied, "Well I didn't drive it yet, but I like the way it makes me feel."

Timothy said, "Let's take it for a test drive." Timothy grabbed the keys, put a tag on it, and off they drove. Lela was in love with it. She liked the way it drove; the gas mileage was good; it had her name all over it. After this drive, she knew she would have to whine to her daddy. She bet he was ready for it. She drove back to the dealership.

"Daddy..."

Mr. Daniels replied, "Say no more, pumpkin, I already know you want it. I can hear it in your voice."

Timothy said, "Let's crunch some numbers, shall we? Ticket price with taxes... the total will be $62,975. With my discount, we can knock it down to $53,000."

Mr. Daniels replied, "Is there someone else's discount we can use with yours to knock it down some more?" Timothy laughed; Mr. Daniels didn't. Lela giggled. Mr. Daniels said, "Okay, here's what we are going to do. I will put twenty-five grand down on the car; that should knock her payments down to ten dollars a month, right?" Timothy gave that SMH look.

Mr. Daniels said, "Lela, it's up to you. If you want to pay the rest on a monthly payment, you can do that, or pay the balance out of your trust fund."

Lela said, "I have a trust fund?"

Mr. Daniels replied, "Since birth."

"How much is in it?"

"Enough!" Mr. Daniels replied. "We had that for your college, your condo, and we'll use it when you get married. That's what it was set up for."

Lela asked Timothy, "How much would my payments be?"

Timothy replied, "The usual five-year loan would be $528 a month. "The more you pay, the quicker you can pay it off."

Lela said, "And I'll do just that. I'll make the monthly payments; that way I can build my credit."

"I raised a smart girl."

Lela replied, "You sure did, Daddy." Mr. Daniels wrote out the check; Lela signed the papers, and Timothy handed her the keys.

Timothy said to Lela, "So I will see you Sunday, Lord willing?"

Lela replied, "Looking forward to it." Lela drove her daddy to his car, and she followed him home. Her mom was waiting outside to see Lela's car.

Mrs. Daniels said, "Oh, Lela, that is definitely you."

Lela replied, "I know, Mommy, I love it."

Mr. Daniels said, "You take good care of this car. It's a good investment; you treat it like one."

"I definitely will, Daddy. Thank you so much."

Mr. Daniels replied, "For you, Sunshine, anything."

Sunday morning, Lela headed to church. When she walked in, she didn't want to bring notice to herself, so she sat in the back. As soon as she sat down, Timothy tapped her on the shoulder.

"I'm glad you made it. Would you like to move up a little closer?"

"Not really."

Timothy replied, "Oh please, you must." She grabbed her bag and moved up closer. Service started promptly at ten o clock. The little children sang praise and worship, and it was beautiful. Lela enjoyed that. After worship was over, she saw one of the older youths bring out a chair, front and center. Timothy said, "We have a special guest, we would like to do a presentation to her." Timothy stepped off the podium and walked over to Lela. He grabbed her hand and escorted her to the chair.

"What is this about?"

"You'll see." Lela saw a group of teenagers coming down the aisle in single file with gifts in their hands. The first one had a photo album and handed it to Lela. She opened it. There were pictures from all the years she worked at the camp. All of the children she had watched were now teenagers. There were pictures of them at the park having water balloon fights, barbecues, finger painting, arts and crafts. The pictures showed her reading and taking naps with them. In one picture, she was combing a little girl's hair, while another little girl was combing Lela's.

They had brought all kinds of gifts and put them beside her. Timothy said, "They have been asking for you for years, and I've been trying to track you down. You showed them love and compassion, and they never forgot it, so today they want to say thank you." Each of them gave her a hug and kiss. When they said their names, she remembered every one of them. She adored them, and they adored her as well.

After service, Lela thanked Timothy and said, "I didn't see this coming"

Timothy replied, "That's what happens when you do good to others. It comes right back to you. Unexpected appreciation: you don't look for it, but it comes at the right time. It was your time, and now, Ms. Lela, I would like to take you out for dinner. Afterward, maybe we can hang out from time to time and catch up."

"I would like that."

Timothy said, "Let's swing by and pick up your parents. I owe your dad a good grip handshake.

Lela laughed and said, "I'm the hugger. My Daddy, yeah he's a real gripper."

Timothy replied, "One day I'll see if your hugs are as tight as your Daddy's handshakes."

SPONTANEOUS LOVE

As Victor rode by the house at 9:00 pm, there was not a light on anywhere, no car in the driveway. The garbage was set out to be picked up, but the house was dark. Victor didn't want to walk up to the house; the motion detector would come on, and he didn't want to be seen. He parked his car across the street and waited to see if there would be any movement, if a light would come on or something. He waited for an hour, and nothing changed, so he decided to go home. He couldn't call her; she'd mailed him back the phone he brought her, smashed up into little pieces; it looked like she put it through a metal shredder. In the morning, he would go back to her house.

Friday morning on his way to work, Victor rode by the house again. He saw someone on the lawn, so he stopped and got out. It wasn't who he'd expected it to be. A gentleman with a For Sale sign in his hand was getting ready to put it up in front of the house. Victor asked, "This house is for sale?"

"Yes," the gentleman replied. "Are you looking to buy a house?"

"No, I'm looking for the owner who used to live here."

"Oh, I can't help you with that information; I'm a realtor, not a detective."

"The way I'm feeling right now, I don't need your sarcasm," Victor said.

"Sorry you don't have a sense of humor."

"No need to apologize; it's not your fault," Victor replied.

"Sir, you look like you have something on your mind. You care to share? By the way, my name is Richard." Richard reached out his hand to shake Victor's.

"Nice to meet you, Richard. My name is Victor. I don't think you can help me."

"Young man, I am a wise man and probably a number of years older than you. When I sense something, nine out of the ten times I am right. Who is she, and what didn't you do?" Victor had a look of shock on his face.

"What makes you think it's about a woman?"

"Well, is it about a man?"

Victor laughed. "No, sir, it's not about a man. Her name is Vivian. I would love to stay and chat with you about this, but I was on my way to work, and I don't want to be late."

Richard handed him his card, and said, "When you are ready to talk, here is my number. Give me a call." Victor thanked him, headed back to his car and drove to work. On the way, Victor had two things on his mind: where was Vivian, and how did Richard know what was on his mind? Was it so obvious? What did he know?

He was going to find out soon how much Richard knew about him.

Victor got to work, grabbed Richard's card off the seat, and went in to start the day. Victor was an investigative journalist; he wrote articles on crime. It was very detailed work, and he did it to perfection. Now, he had his work cut out for him. He had some investigating to do – it had nothing to do with his job. He needed to find Vivian.

Victor had met Vivian on the dance floor at a masquerade party. She was dancing when Victor accidentally stepped back and bumped into her. He said he was sorry, and she pushed him and walked away. He stepped on her long dress, so she couldn't move; her body jerked. He pulled her back and said, "Apologize to me."

Vivian said, "For what? You bumped into me."

"It was an accident. I said I was sorry. You had no right to push me, so apologize."

"I will not; you need to watch where you are going." She snatched away from him and walked out to the patio. He waited a couple of minutes, proceeded in that direction and pushed her. "OMG," she said, and SPLASH, she fell into the pool. Her mask came off; she was beautiful.

Victor said, "Oh, there is beauty under that mask, beauty with an ugly attitude. While you're in there, scrub off the attitude, please. I can throw you some soap. Now can I get my apology?" She shoved some water at him and said, "There's your apology."

Victor said, "You should have worn a mule's mask to this party, as stubborn as you are."

"Well, apparently you're the ass, and you don't need a costume for that."

"Apparently, I don't," Victor said. He walked away and left her in the pool. She swam to the edge and climbed out. She looked around for him. He had left the party, and she couldn't enjoy the rest of the evening soaking wet, so she left as well. As she walked outside, Victor was right there with a towel. "Can we call a truce now?" he asked.

"Do I have a choice?" Vivian replied. Victor slowly walked around her, and then he leaned up against his car.

"Why did you walk around me?"

"I wanted to see if there was a nice bone in that fine body of yours. Why do you have to be so mean?"

"I'm mean because I choose to be."

"Do you know me personally?" Victor asked.

"No, I don't."

"Why do you have an attitude with me? Have I done anything to you, besides baptize you in the water, which it looks like you may need a double dose of?" She smiled. "I don't believe it, you smiled, and it's a pretty one too. Maybe we can put off the baptism for another time. Hello, my name is Victor."

"Please to meet you, Victor. My name is Vivian."

"It is very nice meeting you, Vivian."

"I should have an attitude with you; you pushed me in the water."

"Well, you looked like you were steaming, and you needed to cool off. I did apologize after bumping into you, guess that wasn't good enough."

"It's not you, Victor, and I shouldn't take it out on you, so I do apologize. I should have done that from the beginning."

"Apology accepted. I do owe you some dry clothes. I have a pair of sweatpants and a t-shirt, and I just picked them up today." He grabbed the bag out of his car and handed it to her; she went inside to change. When she came back out, she looked like a model. The heels she had on topped it off. He said, "Oh, you make a wife beater look so sexy."

"Thank you. I would like to return these items to you, so if you give me your number, I will make sure you get them back." She turned on her phone. It was dead, and she tried again – nothing.

Victor said, "What's wrong with your phone, does it need a charge?"

"No, I think you killed it."

"How is that possible?"

"It was fully charged when you pushed me in the water. I had my phone in my pocket, and it got wet, so I think it's dead. My phone is not waterproof."

"Oh, I see. Let it sit in some rice tonight. If that doesn't work, I'll give it the proper burial, and buy you another one."

"Thank you. I would appreciate that."

"Do you need a ride home?"

"No, I have a car, but thank you."

"Okay, well then, I'll say goodnight to you and look forward to talking with you tomorrow."

"But I still need your number," Vivian said. Victor got a permanent marker from his briefcase and told her to turn around; he wrote his number on the back of the t-shirt.

"Now you permanently have my number. Don't wash the shirt, just keep it as a souvenir." They parted ways. Vivian went home and put her phone in rice as instructed. In the morning, she checked her phone; it was still dead. She called Victor to let him know that her phone wasn't working, and she needed a new one. He told her where to meet him; they would pick up one. They met at the store that afternoon. He said, "Pick any phone you want." She looked around and found one she liked.

She asked the salesman, "Is this phone waterproof?"

"Yes, it's waterproof."

"That's good. You never know when someone is going to push you in the water with your phone." Vivian looked at Victor; Victor looked at the wall. Then he turned back to her and started laughing.

Victor asked, "Do you want to keep your same number?"

"No, I can use a new one." The gentleman programmed her phone with a new number and handed it to her. Victor paid for it, and they left the store.

"What are your plans for the rest of the day?" Victor asked.

"I have nothing planned; you want to do something together?"

"Sure, but I had plans to wash my car after I left the store with you," Victor said.

"I'll follow you, and we can wash both our cars, okay?"

"If you're up for the job, let's do it," Victor said. She followed him back to his place. They washed her car first, then his. After he washed it, she rinsed the car and accidentally sprayed him with the water.

Vivian said, "OOPS."

"It's okay, accidents happen," Victor said. While she was still rinsing the car, he went inside the garage. She felt water hit her back. She turned around. He had a super soaker water gun. He sprayed her again, and she took the hose and watered him down. She chased him with the hose, and he shot back with the water gun. They laughed and sprayed water; it was a spontaneous moment, and they loved it. Good thing it was summer, or they would have been icicles. They finished washing the car and then proceeded into the house.

Victor said, "I guess I owe you some more dry clothes." Vivian laughed. He gave her some shorts and a sweatshirt, with a pair of socks.

"What are the socks for?"

"I don't want you to walk on the tile floor barefoot."

"Oh, that makes sense."

"Hand me your clothes, and I'll wash and dry them." She changed her clothes and handed them to him.

"Make yourself at home. The TV remote is on the table; let me get this load of clothes going. I'll be right back." Vivian cozied up with a blanket she took off the back of the couch. She grabbed the remote, turned on the TV and watched it until he came back. He sat on the couch and propped his feet up on the table. Vivian already took up half the couch; she was stretched out.

She said, "Oh, did you want to cozy up on the couch? I'll make room for you."

"No, it's fine; I'm comfortable like this."

"Okay," she said. She stretched and kicked him with her foot. "Oh, I'm sorry, I just needed to stretch."

He grabbed her foot, took off the sock and began to tickle it. She started laughing and kicking him. He got up, and pounced on her and started tickling her in her stomach. She started screaming and laughing. She got up and tried to run, and he grabbed her and tickled her some more. Then he stopped.

She looked at him and said, "What's wrong?"

"I never thought I would have so much fun with you. You're special, Vivian. If I was with anyone else, I would have made love to them, sent them home, and thought no more about them, but you, I can't do that with."

"Well, is there anyone else?"

"There is, but we can be good friends."

"I was hoping you didn't have anyone, but I thank you for your honesty. I can come by and get my clothes some other time. I think I need to go now."

"Please don't go."

"I think it's best that I do." She kissed Victor on the cheek and left. That moment left them without words to say to one another for a month. Then Victor called her to say he needed to see her. She gave him the address; he came over an hour later.

"Hello, Vivian, how have you been?"

"I'm okay, Victor. What did you need to come over to talk about?"

"I came over here because I need to be honest with you; I feel I owe you that."

"You don't owe me anything. We never talked about a relationship or anything; we were just having fun."

"But you felt something that night, didn't you?" Victor asked.

"I did, and that's why I left."

"For some odd reason, I feel I need to explain why I am the way I am, but only to you. I never wanted to say this to any of the other women, but I feel so connected to you."

"What is it that you need to tell me?"

"I really do care for you."

"You could've told me that on the phone."

"I know, but I needed to see your face. I'm cold-hearted, Vivian. I've been hurt, and I made a promise to myself that no other woman was going to hurt me, that I would never love again because I don't trust a woman's heart. I know every woman is different, but I can't take that chance. I get into relationships with a guarded heart and make promises that I don't keep because I don't want to get hurt, so I put women in positions that I don't want to be in. Instead of me getting hurt, they do. I make women feel that they are loved. I love to hear them tell me they are in love with me, when all along I am not sharing my heart with them. I give them good love; they give me their heart, but I'm inconsistent. I do a fade out. I don't call them. They text, and I don't text back, or I may say something they want to hear. They want to see me, and I make excuses. I have their heart, but then I turn a deaf ear to their needs and wants. It boosts my ego to do that. I'm cocky and arrogant. I know I'm handsome, but at the end of the day, I'm lonely because I'm scared to love someone."

Vivian looked a little stunned. "Why are you telling me this?"

"Because being with you made me want to change."

"Change what? I didn't do anything with you."

"No, but you did something to me."

"Are you finished, Victor?"

"Yes."

"Now, let me tell you why I left and why it will never work with us. I am the same way as you are. Yes, I felt something, but being scared, I didn't want to be hurt. I don't sleep around. My body is sacred. I can't turn my feelings on and off like you can. A man makes love to me, that's the man I want to be with forever. That's what I'm saving myself for. I want to be married; I want to fall deeply in love with someone, and I want him to feel something with me he has never felt before. I appreciate you coming by and telling me your heart, but I think it's best that you go. We are not good for one another because we don't want the same thing. Goodbye, Victor."

"But, Vivian—"

"Goodbye, Victor. Please go."

That was three months ago, and now Victor needed to find her because his heart was yearning for her. He left the office and called Richard, asked if they could meet somewhere to talk. Richard said he could meet him for lunch in an hour. Victor finished the article he was working on, sent it to the editor and was on his way. Victor grabbed a seat and waited for Richard, who walked in ten minutes later.

"I didn't expect to hear from you so soon," Richard said.

"My heart is aching. I couldn't go another day without talking."

"What's on your mind, son?"

"I'm in love with the lady I was telling you about, Vivian."

"I can see that."

"I poured out my heart to her. I told her what I was, told her what I didn't want to be anymore. I told her what I wanted to be with her."

"Did you really tell her what she wanted to hear?"

"What do you mean?"

"What did she say to you?" Richard asked.

"She said she wanted to be married. She wants a husband, and she's saving herself for him."

"And what did you say to her?"

"I told her being with her made me want to change."

"Change into what?" Richard asked.

"A better man!"

"I see." Richard was quiet for a couple of seconds, and then he spoke. "A woman hears with her ears, and she speaks from her heart , hoping you can understand what her heart is saying. A woman doesn't like to repeat herself. The words from her heart are valuable; they carry a precious weight. If you do not value what she says, she feels she is not important to you. Whatever you feel in your heart to say to her, give it to her. She'd rather you tell the truth than a lie. Women love hard; they love whole; they love pure, and they love forever. If you are not up for that job, don't string them along. You told Vivian just what you wanted, but you didn't tell her what she wanted to hear.

"You see, son, you told her you wanted to be a better man, and she wanted to hear you say you wanted to be her husband. You didn't listen to what she said because if you had, your response should have been, 'I'm not ready to be a husband.' You weren't listening to her heart; you were just listening. A man who loves a woman dissects her words, plays them over and over in his mind, and when his heart is ready to receive it, he speaks from it. When you are ready to become what Vivian wants, then you will find her, but if you just want to become a better man, then you will lose her. She needs more than a better man; she needs a better man who wants to be her husband. Respect what she wants. You don't play around with that one; her standards are high. If you want to play, find a playmate. Vivian is a woman and is not to be played with. The one you love will be the one you change for. Do you understand, son?"

"Yes, sir, I understand."

"You have a lot to think about. Order some lunch, it's my treat," Richard said. They ordered lunch and continued the conversation. After lunch, Victor headed back to work, and Richard went on to sell some houses. Victor and Richard stayed in touch. They hung out, went to basketball games. Victor needed Richard in his life; he needed to mature in certain areas, and Richard was right there to prune him. Victor started to go to church with Richard. Richard was a deacon at the church. He started to see a difference in Victor's lifestyle, which had changed dramatically. He was more settled. He softened his heart; he didn't date anyone, and he still felt love for Vivian. Victor didn't change for a woman, he changed for himself. He needed that, and he needed to be by himself to see it.

Thanksgiving was approaching. Richard called Victor to see what he was doing for the holiday. Victor said he didn't have any plans. Richard said the family was flying out to Seattle for the holiday, and if he didn't have any plans, would he like to join them? Victor said if it wasn't an inconvenience, he'd be happy to. They were flying out in a couple of weeks. Richard said he would buy his ticket, so they could fly together. Victor said he would reimburse him when he saw him. Victor was excited to meet Richard's family; he'd grown close to Richard, who was like a father to him. Richard always called him "son" and that made him feel even closer. They met at the airport that Wednesday morning. Richard handed Victor his ticket. Victor asked how much he owed him, and Richard said, "This one is on me."

The flight was two hours. They landed and picked up the rental car, then headed to the hotel where they would be staying. They checked in and settled in for the night. Richard knocked on Victor's door.

"I wanted to see if you were settled in, make sure you were okay."

"Yes, sir; everything is fine."

"I want to tell you something, son, I'm really proud of you. You turned your life around, and you did it for you. One day, you will make someone a good husband, but you must want it. You can't be forced into it; it will be your heart's desire. You've matured into a man, and I'm very, very proud of you. I love you, son."

"I love you too, Richard." Richard gave him a hug and went back to his room. Morning came, and they met downstairs for breakfast, Richard told Victor they would be heading out to his aunt's house in a few hours. They chatted, finished breakfast, and Victor went back to his room to find something to wear. He took a nap; when the time came, he got dressed and met Richard downstairs. They piled into the car; it was a thirty-minute drive to their destination. The house was packed with relatives. Victor hadn't known Richard's family was that big. They always had Thanksgiving at Richard's great aunt's house.

The house was huge. Victor felt right at home. Richard introduced Victor to his Great Aunt Cathy and all the family. Cathy was the matriarch; she was ninety-two and beautiful, with white hair in perfect waves and a pumpkin-colored silk blouse.

Everyone was pleased to meet Victor. The table was set: turkey, ham, fried chicken, collard greens, sweet potatoes, potato salad, green beans, cranberry sauce, stuffing – you name it, it was on the table. The pies were cooling on the sideboard; those Aunt Cathy had made with the same recipe she'd used since she was a girl. Everyone sat down. Richard sat at the head of the table, and Victor sat next to him. There was an empty seat next to Victor, but he didn't pay it any mind. Richard was about to say grace when the doorbell rang, Richard excused himself from the table to answer the door. Whoever was at the door was happy to see him. He brought the visitor in the dining room.

Richard said, "I brought someone with me I would like you to meet." Richard walked over to Victor, who had his back to them. Richard said to Victor, "I would like you to meet my daughter." Victor stood up and turned around. It was Vivian. Victor had a look of shock on his face, and Richard wore a big grin—so did Vivian.

"Hello, Victor. It has been a long time; how have you been?"

"I've been good, and yourself?"

"All is well."

"Okay, let's say the blessing over the food so we can eat." Richard said to Vivian, "I saved you a seat next to Victor." She sat down, and Richard began to say grace. After grace, everyone started to dig in, passing bowls, dipping gravy, cutting the turkey, spooning the greens. Plates were filled, mouths were fed; it was a very enjoyable evening. The house was filled with love, laughter, and joy. After dinner, Victor took Vivian into the living room to talk; everyone was quiet, so they could hear.

"Were you surprised to see me?" Vivian asked,

"Very. I had no idea that Richard was your father."

"Yes, he is my father and a very good one at that. He's been telling me you guys have been hanging out; you've become real close to him."

"Yes, he's really helped me in a lot of ways."

"That's awesome; that's good to know."

"I see you sold your home."

"Yes, that had been in the making for a while. I was moving to Seattle before I met you. I didn't leave because of you; I left because I was selling my house. I came here so I could buy the one I'm in now."

"You sent me the phone I brought you. It was in pieces."

"Yes, I apologize for that. As I was moving, I was on the phone upstairs, and it slipped out of my hand and smashed into pieces. I knew I couldn't use it, and I didn't want to throw it in the trash, so I sent it back to you."

His eyes searched hers. "I missed you, Vivian. I missed you so much. My heart has been aching for you. Your father told me when I was ready to become the man that you wanted, I would find you. I found you, I do love you, and I want to marry you."

"Daddy said that you would be ready for me. He said when you look for your wife, you'll find me, and you found me. Yes, Victor, I will marry you."

"I don't have a ring for you; I didn't know you were going to be here."

They heard a voice in the background. "I have one for you."

Aunt Cathy came out with a red velvet box. She said, "This ring had been passed down from generation to generation. Vivian is my favorite great niece, and I held onto this ring for many years. I was going to release this ring to her when the right man came along. Richard has told me so many good things about you, Victor, and I believe you will be the husband that she desires in her heart." Aunt Cathy gave the box to Victor, her delicate old hand resting on his for a moment. Victor opened it up; it was a three-carat diamond ring. He slid it on Vivian's finger, and it fit perfectly.

Victor said, "So let's make it official. Will you marry me, Vivian?"

"Yes, Victor, I will marry you." They sealed it with a kiss.

The house yelled with joy. Richard came and hugged them both. "I'm so happy for the both of you; you are now complete, but no hanky-panky until the wedding night."

"I respect her, Dad; we have a Spontaneous Love. I fell in love with a virtuous woman, and I will wait for that night."

"That's my boy. That's my boy…."

EMPTY HANGERS

Many cold nights I've seen. But not as cold as the night I walked into the house. I called her name. No answer. I walked into the dark bedroom. The only light I saw on was the light in the closet. I walked over and saw all those empty hangers, where her clothes used to be. She was gone. Why would she stay; I didn't treat her like she was my lady. Would I have stayed if she had treated me the same way I treated her? I doubt it. Before I start expressing how I'm feeling now, let me take you back to where all this began.

I met Genevieve some years ago, through a mutual friend. It was sort of a blind date, but I could see clearly that she was fine. We met for dinner. She was classy, and she had a beautiful smile. Everything on her body was proportioned. She wasn't fit but was looking good in all the right places. She licked her lips when she talked and that was a turn-on to me. She'd talk with her eyes. They moved stealthily.

She was my kind of girl. We kicked it. I mean, I still had my other women on the side. But I told her she was my lady. I told her what she wanted to hear. I'm a man; I have no time for commitment. No woman is going to tie me down. I was leading her on to think we were serious. She took the bait. I was reeling her in. She was not letting go. She had a pure heart. I could tell

235

by her conversations how loyal she would be. Yeah, I liked that about her. She could be loyal to me while I still messed around on her.

My women love me. They spoil me. Give me what I want. Who would pass that up? I'm so good at my game. None of the women know about each other. My game is on point. But why am I in my feelings right now, don't want to lose focus, let's stay on track about her. I was enjoying her. She started staying over more, to the point she moved in. I still had my player card. But I was more secretive with it.

Genevieve was everything a man could ever want. I liked what I was doing, and it satisfied me in every way. We'd lie in bed; she'd want to talk about her day and cuddle, and I'd ignore her, turn over and pretend I was asleep. We rarely had sex anymore, but I still wanted her.

Okay. Let me stop lying. I didn't want her, not the way she thought, but at the same time I didn't want anyone else to have her. She had qualities that were so real. She was a woman. She was all woman. She was like fire. She'd melt you down with her words with her deep, sultry, sometimes raspy voice.

She had a soulful way of getting to you. She was like seasoned collard greens. She had all the ingredients in her— nothing missing—and the taste of her was so delicious, her kisses wet and juicy like a peach. Her lips looked edible. I loved sucking on them. She stood out most definitely. I should've told her I didn't want to be in a committed relationship. Every time she smiled so innocently, I would punk out. She was just too sweet.

One morning on my way to work, I grabbed her phone by mistake. I didn't notice it until after I got to work an hour later. She called to say she was bringing my phone. We swapped them. She kissed me on the cheek. Now here I am, on the floor in the closet, looking up at these empty hangers, reading the letter she left for me.

Much time has been wasted. I knew you were seeing other women; your demeanor showed me that. I saw all I needed to in your phone. I saw the pictures, text messages and videos. I hope you're happy with yourself, what you're doing, and the road you're going down. You will be lonely for the rest of your life. You don't deserve a good woman—you don't deserve a woman at all. Goodbye.

I tried calling her. Her number was disconnected. I found out from a friend, she moved out of town. Why was I feeling like I loved her? Why was my heart beating so fast? No woman has ever made my heart beat like this. I disrespected her on so many levels. She didn't deserve that. She was treasure, and I treated her like trash. I had to find her. I searched for her, to no avail. I couldn't find her.

No one would give me information on her. No address, number, nothing. She had every right for me not to know where she was; I couldn't be mad at her. I don't believe I'm going to say this; I'm in love with her. There, I said it. She wouldn't

237

believe me if I told her now. I gave up all the women. It's funny, but not. I couldn't give them up when she was here, but I gave them up, and now she's gone.

What a fool I was, thinking I could have it both ways.

Months went by. I was still calling her phone. Still disconnected. A week later, I found out she didn't move out of town; she moved out of state. She got a promotion, and her job moved her to New York.

She sent me a postcard saying, "Hope all is well. I know your birthday is coming up. I'll be in town, would like to take you out for dinner. See you soon."

She made my day. In a couple of weeks, she'd be here. She confirmed the address and time we would meet. I knew I was going to win her back. She was so beautiful and sexy, and I was going to tell her that. She was everything I wanted; I was going to tell her that too. I made sure I looked good that night. Clean cut, new fit. I wore the cologne she liked. I bought her a dozen pink roses. She'd like those; they're her favorite. I hoped she was as anxious to see me as I was her.

I showed up at 8:00 pm sharp. I walked in, checked on the reservations, and the waitress took me to my table. I was looking around to see if I could see any sign of her. I was fidgeting in my seat. I couldn't wait to see her. I had so many things to tell her. At 8:15pm, I saw this silhouette of a woman—the body on this woman! She looked like she been to all the gyms, tight and right, but my focus was on Genevieve. I had no time to be looking at someone else.

I saw her walk over to the waitress. My eyes were drawn to her. They couldn't stop looking at her. The waitress pointed in my direction, and that sexy silhouette was slowly walking towards me. It couldn't be. Wait, I knew that walk! She arrived at my table and said, "Hello, stranger."

It was Genevieve! Oh, how I missed that raspy, sultry voice. My heart sunk. I hugged her so tight.

Genevieve said, "Your hug feels like somebody missed me."

I didn't want to let her go. I kissed her on the cheek, pulled out her chair. I handed her the roses, and she smelled them.

She said, "You remembered they are my favorite."

I said, "I remember a lot of things." I went on to say how sorry I was, that I was such a fool to let her go, that I'd given up women and my cheating ways, how much I missed her. I said I was in love with her. Everything I rehearsed in my mind, I told her. She had this nonchalant look on her face, like SO! I went on and on about how my life was without her. How much she meant to me. Her facial expression never changed from the "SO?" look.

Genevieve said, "It's good to hear all that, but I needed to hear this when I was with you. Perfect timing isn't now, it was back then. You can't change what happened. You can't take me back and retrieve wasted time. What I lost, you can't give me back. You can't give me back my tears I cried; you can't give me back my feelings or take away the pain you caused. It's too late for how you feel now. Why should I care about how you feel now, when you didn't care about how I felt then? What makes your feelings so much better than mine? I loved you for so long thinking we had something going on. You lured me into your web and kept me there panting for you. The way you saw me then, and the way you see me now—I'm the same woman. Why change now? You can't give me back what I lost. I lost a piece of myself. That's irreplaceable, but some things can be replaced."

She looked down at her phone; texted something and continued the conversation. "What you're telling me now I needed to hear back then." Next thing I know a gentleman walked up to our table, grabbed a chair and sat down. He kissed Genevieve on the cheek and said, "Hey, baby, sorry I'm late, had to find a parking spot." He took her hand and slid two sparkling rings on her finger.

"You left your wedding rings on the dresser."

She smiled at him like she used to smile at me. "Thank you, baby, I forgot to put them back on after I lotion my hands." She turned to me and said, "I'd like for you to meet my husband, Jonathan. You see, Greg, if my heart had never broken by you, my husband wouldn't have ever found me, so we came here to say thank you, Happy Birthday. Order anything on the menu, Jonathan will gladly pay for it. It's the least he can do for his good fortune that you let me go."

I felt so humiliated and embarrassed, but I deserved that. Would I take me back? I don't think so. Genevieve got up to use the rest room. My eyes followed her, but his eyes were dead on mine. I cleared my throat and said to him, "You have a good woman."

He said, "I know, that's why I married her. Too bad you never appreciated her the way I do."

Yup, I deserved that too. The night ended fairly well, though every look she gave him, every smile...well, it seems a heart can break over and over. They were heading back to New York in the morning. I came home disgusted at myself for letting someone like her go. There will never be another one like her; she is irreplaceable. These empty hangers will always remind me of her and this closet will be just like my heart...empty.

To Be Continued

KISS OF LIFE

As the moving van pulled off, Genevieve closed the door, turned around and looked at all the boxes she had to unpack. She sat on the floor and opened up a box. It was full of photo albums with pictures of empty promises; she threw them to the side, the box as well. She started unpacking the other ones. She hung up her pictures, moved the furniture to its proper spot, put up her dishes, and made up all the beds. She unpacked from sun up to sun down. She came into the living room, after pouring herself a glass of wine, and cozied up by the fireplace. The box she threw to the side was staring at her.

She sipped her wine. The crackling sound of the fireplace was soothing. Her phone rang. She looked at the number and let it go to voicemail. She got up, walked over to the box, put the photo albums in it, walked it out to the garbage and put the box in it. She lay on the couch and watched the fire. Her phone rang again. She answered it but didn't say hello. She heard the voice on the other line saying, "Hello. Hello? Genevieve, are you there? I'm sorry, baby, please talk to me." She hung up the phone and turned it off.

She put the fire out, went up to her room, put her wedding rings on the dresser, sat on her bed, turned on her laptop, and checked her email. She had five emails from Jonathan. She didn't open them. She checked her other email. Another email came in from him. She ignored it, closed her laptop, she laid down and closed her eyes while a teardrop rolled down her face and hit the pillow, she cried through the night. She thought about opening the emails, thought about turning her phone on to check the voicemails. She always thought about Jonathan, and his best interests. All Jonathan thought about was how many lies he was going to tell her.

Genevieve had moved to New York a year ago. Her job had a promising position for her that fell through after six months; she met Johnathan at the grand opening of the franchise and fell in love after dating for two months. Johnathan was a smooth talker; everything he said sounded promising, just because of the tone in his voice. Genevieve believed him enough to marry him. He said they would buy a house. That fell through because though he said he had good credit – said his credit score was 850 –it turned out to be 580. She thought there was no way he could have dyslexia with his credit score, so she started doing some research on him.

She managed to get his Social Security number because she knew his birthday. When she did the research, she was blown away. He was still married to someone in Connecticut, not divorced yet, *still married,* and behind in child support. He had told her he didn't have any children. He had credit cards that he was behind on, eviction notices from two apartments for non-payment – the list went on and on. There were even lies in her wedding rings. She hadn't had her rings two months when one of the stones came out. She went to a jeweler to get another put in,

243

and they said we can put a new diamond in, but it will look odd with cubic zirconia.

The stones were fake and so was the man she was married to. After she found out all the information, when Johnathan went out of town for business, she packed up and left. Rather, he said he went out of town for business; he had gone out of town to see his other wife. Genevieve had a trace on his phone, and the locator put him in Connecticut. She had her friend Carlos call him. Carlos first called Genevieve and then Jonathan. Genevieve put her phone on mute.

Jonathan answered and said, "Hello."

"Hello, may I speak to Jonathan."

"This is he."

Carlos said, "Hello, sir, this is the New York Fire Department. I'm calling to inform you that we put a fire out at your house; apparently, there were some clothes out in the front of your house. We got there quickly to put it out before it damaged your home."

Johnathan replied, "Fire in front of my house! Is my house okay!"

"Yes, sir, your house is fine."

Johnathan said, "You said clothes. Who did they belong to?"

"Apparently they were yours."

"How do you know they were mine?"

Carlos answered, "Because I saw your wife bring them out of the house and set them on fire. After we roasted our marshmallows over them, we put the fire out."

Johnathan said, "What are you talking about Marshmallows? My wife did what?"

"Wife...hmm...which wife are you referring to, the one in New York, or the one in Connecticut?"

"I only have one."

Carlos said. "Well, the court documents say you have two wives."

Jonathan replied, "How did you get all this information about me?"

"I am best friends with your wife Genevieve, who has been listening to our conversation the whole time; she was nice enough to give me the information, so I could relay it to you."

"I don't believe you."

Genevieve took her phone off mute and said, "Do you believe him now?" You could hear a pin drop all the way in Connecticut. It was silent for about ten seconds. She then said, "I know you're with your wife. The locator on your phone puts you there. I don't know the reason why you're there, and there's no need to tell me. I've decided to move back to Chicago. I'm leaving today. You can stay where you are; the house is empty. Legally, we are not married because you are still married to her. Goodbye, Jonathan." Click, she hung up the phone.

Carlos got up from the couch, walked over to Genevieve and said, "Are you okay?"

"I'll be fine; I always bounce back. Thank you for driving to New York to help me move. I owe you big time."

He replied, "Anytime."

That was three months ago. She had had enough of men with their straight-faced lies. She was enjoying being back in Chicago. New York was fun and exciting, but she missed home. One thing New York did do for her was open up a different side of her. Jonathan took her to an open mic club one night, where they did creative art. Some spoke it; others showed visual art. She heard a poet that night who spoke profundity. It unlocked something in her. She took a ladle and scooped up some of her emotions, mixed them with some rhythm, contouring, making a poetic ombre, and glossed it all with the color of love. She liked the formula she was creating. What she wanted to say was not for the man she was supposedly married to; it would marinate until it was time to spill out into the heart it was made for.

Back in Chicago, she recalled old memories. She didn't want to reminisce, rehearse, or replay the events, so she walked away from them. It was Friday night, rainy and warm. Crystal, Genevieve's best friend, called her. Crystal said, "Hey, G, what are you doing?"

"Nothing. It's raining out. Who wants to go out in this weather?"

"Well, have you been out anywhere since you've been back in Chi town?"

"I've been lying low since I've been here. Don't want too many people to know I'm back."

"People or a person?" Crystal didn't hear a response. "Genevieve you there?"

"Yes, I'm here."

"Okay, you got quiet on me."

Genevieve replied, "I'm sorry; I put the phone down. I thought I told you to hold on." She'd heard what Crystal said; she just didn't want to respond.

Crystal said, "You need the Kiss of Life."

"What is that?"

"Listen to Sade, listen to what she says. I'll swing by and pick you up in an hour." Click, they hung up. Genevieve grabbed her earphones, looked up "Kiss of Life." She loved the intro. She walked over to the window; saw the full moon and the rain. She set the scene in her mind, closed her eyes and listened to every word. She was feeling what she felt in New York; a heatwave of passion went through her soul. It was heating up all that was marinating in her. She didn't know it yet, but there was a thirsty soul out there, and she was going to drench it like a waterfall hitting a scorched ground for the very first time.

Beep, beep. Crystal beeped her horn, and she ran out to the car. Crystal said, "I talked with Carlos; he said he would hang out with us."

"Hanging? Where are we going?"

"What are you in the mood for?"

"How about Karaoke?

247

Crystal replied, "The only time I sing is in the shower, and the last time I checked they don't have showers on stage, so that will be a no for me."

"Surprise me then."

"Carlos works at this bar on East Fifty-fourth St. We can hang there for a few until he gets off, then wherever we go, we can ride together."

"Okay, that's fine." They drove to the bar. It was pouring rain. They got out of the car, ran inside quickly, shook off the water and walked in. They looked for Carlos. They walked over to the bar and sat down. They greeted him. He leaned over and kissed the girls on the cheek.

Carlos said, "So, what are we doing tonight?"

"It's raining out. I really don't want to be in and out of the rain."

Carlos replied, "Well, I knock off in thirty minutes. If you guys want to hang around here until it stops, we can do that."

They thought that was a good idea. Genevieve looked around. There were very few customers in the place, especially for a Friday night. She said, "Why is it so dull in here? This looks like it should be a hot spot."

Carlos said, "It used to be full at one time, but we can't find any entertainment. We play music, but people just drink and mingle."

Genevieve asked, "What's the stage for?"

"We used to have a live band, but since people aren't coming in as much, we can't afford to pay them." Thunder and lightning accompanied with more rain wasn't favorable weather for them, so they stayed at the bar.

Genevieve said, "Let's revive this place."

Carlos asked, "How?"

"Do those mics work?"

"I can turn them on."

She walked up to the stage, grabbed a stool, tapped the mic, and said, "Hello, out there, my name is Genevieve. I just want to say a little something to you tonight, just for fun. I call this 'My best friend.'

Best friends are forever
I think of you
And all the days we have spent together
You are my best friend, my soul mate
And I know you will always be there until the end

Your shoulder to cry on will always be there
Whenever there is something wrong
When times are tough, you are always there
It shows me your love and that you care

Although we are going our separate ways
You will always remain in my heart

None in this world can see

How special you are to me

You are my strength, you are my power

My best friend, my soul mate

I always dreamed of a friend like you

And when I found you, it was like a dream come true

You understand the worst side of me

That no one can ever see

You are the best person I've ever known

My best friend, my soul mate

Is it always that

Together we party and together we cry

We keep our every secret

And cover each lie

Cause we are best friends till the day we die

A friend like you is hard to find

You were always there when no one cared

We have been through good and bad times

And you always made me laugh when I was sad

My best friend, my soul mate

Best friends are like flowers, like a rose

Or like a ghost whose spirit never dies

You are always behind me whenever times are tough
My best friend, my soul mate

You are like a ray of sunshine
Always present with me whenever the world is dark
You have guided me through bad times
Wiped away my tears
My best friend, my soul mate

We are like two bodies and one soul
You are the best person amongst the rest
Our time together is passing day by day
But now until the very end
You will always be there
My best friend, my soul mate

Crystal videotaped her as she spilled out her feelings into the bar. The audience stood up and clapped. Carlos hadn't seen anything like that before. Genevieve stepped off the stage, and people walked up to her and told her how much they enjoyed her. They felt what she was saying. She thanked them and walked back to the bar and sat down.

Crystal said, "You've been hiding this from me?"

"It'd been hidden from me too. I discovered it in New York. This is my first time expressing it; you could call it my debut." Unbeknownst to Genevieve, an old friend was listening in a dim corner. While people were still approaching her, telling her how much they enjoyed her, he slipped away into the storm. It had stopped raining; his storm was regret.

Carlos said, "Girl, you're gifted. You should come back and do this next Friday. I'll talk with my manager and see if it will be okay. Okay, he said it's okay."

Genevieve laughed. "I didn't see you ask anyone."

"I am the manager, I just got promoted tonight."

Crystal said, "Then why are you behind the bar making drinks?"

"For one, Crystal, I'm the mix master; I make the best drinks. Two, my bartender called out sick, so I'm covering this side. That's what good managers do; they fill in spots to keep things running."

"That makes sense. Congratulations on your promotion."

"Thank you, but congrats to you, Genevieve; you may just bring this place to life. We'll call it G on the Mic. Open mic night. Maybe it will bring other talent, but Genevieve is the star."

She smiled and said, "I owe you for coming to my rescue in New York."

He replied, "For you, G, anytime. You didn't belong there. We needed you here; we missed you. I'm glad you came back home." They all did a group hug. It was midnight; they were entertained for the night, and they called it just that. They stayed until Carlos locked up the place. Crystal dropped Genevieve off and then headed home. What Crystal forgot to tell her, is that she had taped her. She put it up on YouTube; she was going to get some hits that would blow her mind.

Saturday morning, Genevieve got a text from Crystal. It said, "Good morning, Star." It had a link attached. She opened it up and saw herself performing last night. She smiled, noting how many had seen her video: five hundred already.

She smiled harder. She called Crystal and said, "Why didn't you tell me you did this last night?"

"I was caught up in the excitement. I totally forgot about it. I knew you wouldn't mind if I submitted it on the tube."

Genevieve replied, "I'm glad you got my good side."

"Girl, with the shape you have, all your sides are good. Did you see all the hits you got?"

"Yes, I've seen them."

"Did you read the comments?"

"No, I just saw the hits. I called you right after I saw the video."

Crystal said, "Read the comments; they are pretty interesting." Genevieve began reading them. They were all positive feedback. She read all the way down to the bottom, and her heart leaped when she read the last one.

It said, "As soon as you spoke into the mic, I recognized your voice. Oh, how I miss that deep, raspy, sultry voice. I enjoyed you on the open mic. Keep up the good work and welcome back home. Sincerely, Greg." A part of her was still in love with Greg. She had been hurt by him but was still in love with him – that was part of her past she didn't want to see again. She called Crystal back.

Genevieve said, "Did you read the comments?"

"I did!"

"Did you read them all?"

"I did!"

"So, you saw what Greg wrote?"

"Yes."

"Why didn't you tell me?"

"I wanted you to see it for yourself. Listen to me for a minute, G. I know you've been hurt by him. Men don't know what they want until they don't have it anymore. They don't realize the value of you until they can't find it in anyone else. I remember when he came asking about you, when you moved to New York. He was lost without you. I knew you were in pain. You were healing from your pain, and he was at the beginning stages of his. I don't know where you are at as far as healing; that's why I wouldn't bring up his name. I respect the tenderness of people's hearts, and when they're wounded I add no more sorrow. When you are ready to talk about it, then I will open the floodgates, but other than that, I'll keep quiet."

Genevieve asked, "Well, what do you know."

"I love you, G, but you're still healing. You can't love that pain away. Forgive Greg first, and then love him if that's what your heart wants. The information that I have is about you, not about him. There is a current of love out there that only you and he

254

can be on. It only works if you're going in the same direction. Let him be your wave and you be on the surfboard. Let him support you as you ride the wave. Wherever direction he goes, follow him. He will support you. Let him build the foundation so you can stand strong.

"He knows he's made mistakes. Do I want to say give him another chance? It's not my place to say; I'm not you. You must be ready for that. But I do know love, and that is what he is feeling for you. Although you didn't see it before, he feels what you were feeling. Give it time, think about it. I have a phone call waiting; we will talk later, okay?"

Genevieve said, "Okay." They hung up. Genevieve knew Crystal was right; she had to forgive him, to heal. She couldn't fight what she was feeling, either, but to love right, she had to forgive and trust him. She wanted Greg to love her the way she loved him. She didn't want to be in a relationship, so maybe they could work on a friendship. At least she wouldn't lose him, and they could grow into something mutual.

Carlos called Genevieve. "Hey, G, what's going on?"

"Nothing. What's up with you?"

"Did you see your video on the Tube?"

"Yes, I saw it this morning. It was like five hundred hits."

"What time did you look at it?" Carlos asked.

"About an hour ago."

"Well, it's at fifteen hundred now."

"OMG, are you serious!"

"Yes, I am. You want to come back tonight and go for round two?"

"That would be nice. I like that."

"Awesome. Let me get the word out that you will be performing again tonight and see what kind of crowd we can draw."

"Sounds like a night of fun," she replied.

"I think it will be," Carlos replied. She walked over to her closet to look for something sexy to wear. It was summertime, July to be exact, and the way she felt was the way she wanted to dress: a halter top and jeans, with a pair of heels, simple but sexy. She texted Crystal to let her know what was going on tonight. Crystal texted back that she would pick her up about nine. Open Mic after Dark is what Carlos named it; it didn't start until ten. That would give Genevieve enough time to feel the vibe of the crowd and know exactly what to say to the ears of her listeners.

It was a sweltering summer night. Genevieve started to get ready around eight. After she took a hot shower, she caressed her skin with Oudh, an exotic oil that penetrated the pores of her skin. She put her hair up in a bun, put on her big bamboo earrings, a little make up, eyeliner and lip gloss. Her skin was already glowing; she was like fire, ready to light up the night. At nine sharp, Crystal was outside waiting. Genevieve got in the car. Crystal said, "Oh, don't we look different tonight! And you smell like Oudh. You know I told you that oil is for a special occasion; that is love oil."

Genevieve replied, "I feel different tonight. It's a beautiful summer night, and I feel loved. Tonight, is special."

Crystal replied, "You sound different too."

"Yes, you gave me a lot to think about from our conversation earlier. I'm not scared to give love another chance."

"That's good to hear, G, good to hear." They arrived at the bar. There was not a lot of activity going on outside, but when they walked in, they saw every table was full; even the bar area was full. Crystal and Genevieve walked to the bar where Carlos was.

Genevieve said, "Wow, there is a difference between last night and tonight."

"You think?" Carlos replied.

"Most definitely."

"Well, get a feel of the vibe. I don't know if you want to go around and get acquainted with the audience or just kind of chill until the show starts. It is your stage tonight, G, so you have control of the atmosphere. I'll introduce you, and then they are yours to entertain."

"Just like that, Carlos?"

"Just like that, G."

"Well, in that case, can I have a glass of sangria? I'll just sit and relax until it's time." Genevieve looked around. It was a happier crowd. They looked eager tonight, like they were expecting something. She saw how couples were interacting with each, the touching of hands, the body language of love; it was a passionate atmosphere. She could smell the scent of love. She loved the way the aroma smelled; the heat was sensual. Although it was cool inside, the passion made the temperature rise. Genevieve handed Carlos a CD. She said, "After I finish the poem, play this."

It was ten o'clock. Carlos went on stage and said, "Good evening, welcome to Open Mic after Dark. My name is Carlos; I want to introduce your hostess, my good friend Genevieve. She will be your entertainer for tonight. I hope you enjoy her; let's welcome her with some love. Hands clap as she walks up to the stage." Carlos dimmed the light in the audience, and a string of white lights across the top of the stage came on.

Genevieve said, "Welcome again to Open Mic after Dark; it is a pleasure to be on this stage tonight. I see lovers out there. How many are married?" Half of the room raised their hands. "How many are moving that way?" Other hands were raised. "What a great vibe I'm getting from the room; I can feel the pulse of passion. You guys love deeply; I like that. While you are in love, you must feed it. Each one of you hungers for it. Never starve each other of what each one deserves. Keep the fire burning; never let it go out.

"Tonight's poem is called 'Remind Me.'

Your sexy hands run along my spine
Remind me, baby, that you are mine
Do those things you do so well
Make me remember why I fell
So hard, so deep

So fast, so steep

You rock me sensually

My body keeps

Craving you, baby, more and more

What you do to me I simply adore

I want you, I need you

Oh, so much

Keep it coming, baby

Your sensuous touch

After you there can be no other

It's you and me

Gloriously smothered

In love, in passion

So incredibly fine

Your sexy hands

Along my spine

Yes, you remind me, baby

That you are mine

So sexy, so passionate

Simply divine.

"Thank you."

The crowd went wild, whistling and clapping, shouting, "Encore, encore!" Then the music played. It was Sade's "Kiss of life," all music, no words. Genevieve had the audience in a tranquil state. As she was singing, out of the dimly lit corner, Greg appeared, and he stood there for her to see. She began to sing, "When I was led to you/ I knew you were the one for me/I swear the whole world could feel my heartbeat/ When I lay eyes on you/ Ahhhh/ You wrapped me up in /The color of love/ You gave me the kiss of life..." People from the audience began to get up and dance to her groove. The atmosphere was seductive. Genevieve sung out of her soul, and you felt the love in her voice. Greg was feeling in his soul what she was singing out of hers. When the song had come to an end, the audience applauded. Greg walked up to the stage and reached for her hand, and she stepped down.

Greg said to Genevieve, "If you are finished here, I'd like to take you somewhere." Crystal blew kisses to them as they left the bar. Greg took her back to his place. He stopped by the kitchen and made a drink, and then they proceeded to the bedroom. He opened the closet door where the empty hangers were, just the way she left them.

"When you left me, Genevieve, my soul was so empty. I was lost. You were my life, and I didn't even know it. I hungered for your touch for so long. I didn't know you had me like that until I didn't have you anymore. I am so sorry I hurt you, baby. I know how much you mean to me now. I want to make a vow to you; I promise to never hurt you again. The pain I felt, I swear I don't want to feel that anymore. I know how you felt. I needed to feel it and I did.

"We need to build a foundation, baby, and it needs to be concrete. I can't live without you, Genevieve. I need you in my life. You are the very air that I breathe. I was suffocating without you."

Genevieve replied, "It feels good to know that what I was feeling, you are feeling now. Not the pain, Greg, but the love. We have gotten beyond the pain and developed a bond that can't be broken. I will be your friend. What we are feeling now is the power of love, we must respect it, and the heart and person it comes from.

Greg walked up to Genevieve and kissed her on her neck. "OMG, you smell so good; does your entire body smell like this?"

She smiled and said, "What do you think?" It started to thunder and then rain. He turned on the radio. "Anytime, anyplace" by Janet Jackson was playing. He untied her halter top, lifted it over her head and laid her on her stomach. He took an ice cube out of the glass and slowly slid it down her back. Her moans excited him. He let the ice cube melt in the center, and he licked the puddle. She clenched the sheets with her hands. He turned her over, drank the rest of his drink, put the ice cube in his mouth, and transferred it to her with a seductive kiss. It was the Kiss of Life, cool, refreshing. It was oxygen, mouth to mouth on impulse.

He looked into her eyes and said, "I want to explore your entire body tonight, baby. I want to touch and taste you."

To be continued

THANK YOU

For all those who have taken the time out to read my thoughts on paper, I thank you. This is my very first book I have written, and I am glad to share it with you. Hopefully you didn't fall asleep reading it. Are you using the book as a coaster yet, do I have a ring on my forehead, or maybe you're using it to hold up the end of the table to balance it? Please laugh; I am.

I wrote this book thinking about you, what you would like to read, do you like suspense, are you on the edge kind of readers. I wrote to keep you wanting more, stirred up. I am starting another book, so look out for it. I couldn't stop at this one. For those that know me, you may see some of my sarcasm in the stories; I'm known for that. For those that don't, this is who I am.

Short and Sassy is just what my book is about – short stories with a sassy twist. I'm short and sassy; well, I'm not short, I just don't have long legs. If you can give me your feedback on how you liked the stories, I would appreciate it. You may have a favorite story; maybe it's all of them. You might want to know how I came up with the title of a story, or tell me what you liked about it, or you may just want to vent because you found yourself in the story. Your feedback keeps me writing. For those that printed my story every time I finished one, I promise to restock the paper in the printer.

AUTHOR BIO

Erica Thomas was born and raised in Philadelphia, Pa. She now resides in Clearwater, Fl. She was given the nickname Ricki as a child; family and friends still call her that today. She has unique ways about herself, even in the distinctive way she walks. The stories in her collection, *Short and Sassy*, have stayed with her for years on end. It's her very reality fused with her imagination; linked by a unity of where it all took place – in Maryland, inside a red brick house with a circular driveway. Every story written was erected out of this house. The layout of the house made the stories surreal.

She has traveled down the road of hurt, pain and disappointment; in the midst of being shattered and broken, her conclusive determination was to never settle for less. In her progression, she has developed to become the woman she is today. Now…she is ready to inspire others.

She desires to minister the Gospel of Jesus Christ in a way that touches their hearts, she wants to encourage, support and assist in the healing of the broken- hearted. Because of her heart to help people, she sees herself as a river which flows into many areas to fulfill the thirst of those who are craving more of who they are. Her dialogue to the world is: "It's time to think differently; step back, see the whole picture because you are looking at it the wrong way; you can move on in spite of your scars!"

263

Erica loves music, especially Smooth Jazz, which inspires her to write. (She is presently writing a Part 2 of Short and Sassy!) She desires to travel the world, teaching women to trust themselves, to believe they could love again and most of all, guard your heart but not enough to miss love.